FIT

Book Four in the Chloe
Daniels Mysteries

By

Deidra D. S. Green

Celebrated Author of Sick,
Sicker, Sickest

FIT: A Chloe Daniels Mystery

Copyright 2017 Deidra D. S. Green

RATHSI Publishing, LLC

www.rathsipublishing.com

ISBN#: 978-0-9977168-9-4

Acknowledgments

I love my reading family and I appreciate you all being with me once again on this crazy journey! I appreciate your willingness to keep reading with me, enjoying these insane characters, and waiting anxiously for the next book. It is a great feeling to know that someone is looking forward to what it is you have to say... well... what these crazy characters have to say. Thank you...

I must thank the Creator from whom all blessings flow. I count it a blessing every time He gives me the opportunity to do what I love. Thank you to my literary team for supporting me in this process. Without your input, diligence, and hard work, none of this would be possible.

Thank you to my friends and family who continue to pray for me, cover me, and keep me lifted up. I can't do this without you. Thank you to the two people who make my life worthwhile, my most precious gifts, VcToryann C'Mone, and Kamerron DeAnthony Alexander. I tell you all the time, I love you. I mean it. You are the reason I do it. I love you beyond the moon and stars... I love you to life...

Dedication

This book is dedicated to everyone who loves a good mystery, laced with intrigue, a bit of romance and a whole lot of crazy...

Chapter One

The house at 3562 Monument Road burned fast. The older shotgun home with antiquated electrical wiring and rotten wood was no match for the gasoline infused fire. It was only when the fire at Mayven's childhood home threatened to incinerate a neighboring home was the fire department called. Nobody in the neighborhood cared if Jerome Mickens house burned down. He didn't deserve to call it his anyway. For the families on Monument Road, that house would always be Melody and her baby girls' house. The fact that he lived there long after Melody and her daughter were gone was an insult to the neighborhood. They considered Jerome a trespasser and a transgressor. So they watched, much like Major and Mayven, as the house was consumed by fire. They didn't like Jerome or his damn dog anyway.

"All rise," the bailiff instructed.

"The Honorable Judge Ruth M. Bledsoe presiding."

The chains on Anna Black clanked as she rose to her feet. The black and white striped prison uniform she wore swallowed her thin frame. Her inmate number was stamped on her back in large block lettering. Dr. Daniels looked over at her. Anna looked some better, not markedly so, however. Prosecutor Norwood had been successful in getting an injunction filed to prohibit prison psychiatrist, Dr. Culpepper, from his experimental medication regiment.

He was well aware who the true author of the injunction was. Dr. Daniels knew she was not one of his favorite people right now, but she didn't care. Although Anna was an infamous serial killer who wreaked havoc on the lives of many people, she still deserved to be treated like a human being, not a guinea pig. Chloe would always stand up for that and stand up to anyone who infringed upon the rights of others.

The Honorable Judge Bledsoe entered the courtroom. Her pristine black robe set her apart as the woman in charge. Her posture and demeanor made everyone in the courtroom take note. Ruth Bledsoe was a seasoned criminal attorney before being appointed to the bench. She had a reputation for being a beast when it came to cross-examination. Her open and closing arguments were legendary and frequently used as exemplary examples in law schools around the country. Ruth M. Bledsoe, Esquire, was ruthless; pun intended.

"You may be seated," Judge Bledsoe announced.

Anna followed the judge's instruction. As she did, Anna looked around for familiar faces in the gallery. When she landed on the faces of her parents, Anna smiled and settled into her seat. Peter and Carrie were two of only a few sitting on the defense side. Those that filled in the seats behind them were mostly media personnel. In preparation for the trial, Judge Bledsoe prohibited the use of cameras or recording devices in the courtroom.

The media were allowed to sit in the gallery but were restricted to the last two rows on either side. If available seats were needed for others intent on being party to the trial, the media would have to give up their seats. Judge Bledsoe hadn't made any friends with the press with those restrictions, but she was no nonsense and was not inclined to be pressured by the media.

"Are we ready to proceed," Judge Bledsoe asked of council.

"Yes, your honor," Prosecutor Norwood answered, standing to her feet.

"Yes, your honor," the public defender replied; half standing, half sitting. Judge Bledsoe took note of his lax posture when addressing her. He wouldn't get away with it a second time. Ethan Ross was overworked and underpaid. After three years in the public defender's office, he was completely burned out. Gearing up for this high profile case was especially challenging. He knew everything he did, say, even down to what he wore would be under a microscope. Conjuring up energy for a case he was destined to lose proved cumbersome for the young attorney.

"If it would please the court, your honor, I would like to make a motion," Prosecutor Norwood announced. Judge Bledsoe looked to the defense table to see if the attorney intended to make an objection. Ross barely lifted his head when Norwood spoke. His defeatist attitude was evident.

"Since there is no objection from the defense, you may proceed." Judge Bledsoe's jab was not lost on anyone in the courtroom with the exception of Attorney Ross.

"Your honor, given that the defendant has admitted to the crimes of which she is convicted, I motion to waive all opening statements as well as testimony and have Anna Black's confession entered into evidence. With that your honor, I would request that the jury be dismissed, and the verdict be left to you to determine based on the evidence presented."

If there were cameras, they would be flashing. This was a pivotal moment, and all eyes were on Judge Bledsoe. An audible gasp went through the crowd. Reporters madly scribbled into their notebooks, hating the judge even more for not allowing recording devices. Neither Dr. Daniels nor Detective Phillips was surprised by Norwood's posturing. She was known for grandstanding. Prosecutor Norwood saw this as her breakout case, and she loved making headlines. Carrie Black, Anna's mother, was visibly shaken by the prosecutor's statement.

It was already hard enough that she'd lost her youngest child. It was even harder to comprehend that her daughter, her flesh and blood, was accused of such horrendous acts. And for the prosecutor to not want Anna to have a fair chance to fight for her freedom? That was nearly more than Carrie could bear. In his usual manner, Peter Black sat there with a blank expression on his face. Unlike his wife, he didn't wear his feelings where they were visible to anyone else. If he were grieving, one would never know it. If he were concerned about Anna, you wouldn't be able to tell that either.

Once again, Judge Bledsoe eyeballed the defense attorney. This time, he felt her piercing gaze. She was practically demanding that he object without verbally instructing him to do so. Attorney Ross begrudgingly got to his feet.

"I object, your honor," he slothfully interjected. Norwood didn't even bother to glance in his direction. He wasn't worthy of her taking note of him.

"On what grounds?" Judge Bledsoe coaxed.

"On the grounds that uh…"

"Judge Bledsoe," Norwood interrupted. "Clearly counsel has no reasonable objection."

"That withstanding, Attorney Norwood, this court will give the attorney an opportunity to speak, and I would caution you to not speak until acknowledged by the bench." Judge Bledsoe was well aware of the ambitious Norwood. Bledsoe would not allow herself to be considered bias or partial because of Norwood's self-serving motives.

"Duly noted, your honor."

Norwood retreated to her seat and perched on the edge; preparing to stand again to counter whatever Ross could come up with.

"You were saying, Attorney Ross," Judge Bledsoe inquired.

"Ah yes, your honor," he stammered. "I object on the grounds that the confession was coerced and my client was not in sound mind at the time that she uh made said disclosure."

"I'm not crazy…"

A hush came over the courtroom as the defendant blurted out.

"Did you just say I'm crazy 'cause I'm not crazy."

Anna looked at her attorney, and when he didn't respond, she took her cuffed hands and pulled at his suit jacket. Murmurs spread across the gallery. Ross slapped at her hands and shushed her. Judge Bledsoe's gavel came down hard against the sound block. Boom, boom, boom.

"Quiet in the courtroom," Judge Bledsoe demanded. Everyone complied except the defendant.

"Judge, I need to talk to you."

"Attorney Ross, please gain control of your client."

Ross sat down next to Anna and implored her to quiet down. He reminded Anna that she couldn't speak directly to the judge without permission. Ross conveyed these instructions in hushed but stern tones. Anna watched him speak, and when he was done, she responded.

"Did you just tell these people I'm crazy? Because I'm not crazy and if you are telling these people I'm crazy, then you are telling a lie. We are in a court of law, and you are not supposed to be dishonest in a court of law. You are supposed to tell the truth, the whole truth, and nothing but the truth so help you, God. If you are lying, then you are not telling the truth." Anna was just as firm in her conviction as her attorney had been. Ross looked exacerbated; not sure what he was supposed to do. The murmuring in the crowd increased by several decibels.

Judge Bledsoe dropped the hammer again.

Boom, boom, boom.

"Attorney Ross, if you cannot gain control of your client, then I will be forced to have her removed from these proceedings."

Ross actually looked relieved at the prospect of no longer having to contend with the unpredictable Anna Black. But before he could address the court, Anna had something else she needed to say. Standing to her feet, Anna addressed the court, over her attorney's meager objection. Now he was the one pulling at her jumpsuit tail trying to get her to sit back down. Anna would not be deterred.

"Your most dubious honor," Anna began, speaking loudly and clearly.

Every effort Ross made to thwart his client were unsuccessful. Prosecutor Norwood jumped to her feet and vehemently objected. This kind of display would not bode well for a conviction. She needed the jury to see Anna as a criminal, not just crazy. Anna refused to be quiet and raised her voice above those who wanted to silence her.

"If this case is about me, I think I should be allowed to speak."

Judge Bledsoe intercepted.

"You have an attorney for that, Ms. Black. He is your representative and should speak on your behalf. You should not be addressing the court directly. Do you understand that?"

"I do, your most high honor," Anna conceded. "However, when the person the state has appointed to represent you is dishonest, do you allow that representation to continue?"

The courtroom quieted down. Ross stood to his feet, trying to make a case for himself and after only a few seconds, Judge Bledsoe struck the mallet definitively and silenced the two of them.

"Ms. Black, I understand you to say you don't feel adequately represented. Is that the case?"

"That's what I am saying your..."

Judge Bledsoe helped up her hand, and Anna obeyed the gesture momentarily.

"A simple yes or no answer would be sufficient, Ms. Black."

"Then, yes."

"Your honor," Prosecutor Norwood spoke.

"You are out of line, Attorney Norwood," Judge Bledsoe scolded. "The next such outburst will result in a sanction, or better yet, a citation of contempt of court." Norwood had no choice but to fall silent.

Detective Phillips smiled. Chloe looked over at him, and they briefly made eye contact. She nudged him with her elbow so he would straighten up. Michael momentarily wiped the smile from his face, but it returned just as quickly. Chloe poked him again but found herself smiling, too. The judge turned her attention back to the defendant.

"Ms. Black, you have the right to a vigorous defense. You also have the right to proper representation. If you don't feel your attorney is working in your best interest, you have the right to request new counsel."

Anna raised her hand like a student in a classroom. Judge Bledsoe indulgently acknowledged her.

"Your most high court judge, does that mean I can fire him?"

"Yes, Ms. Black, you can fire your attorney, but"

Before Judge Bledsoe had a chance to complete her thought, Anna interjected.

"You're fired, mister!"

The courtroom erupted with laughter. There were oohs and aahs in response to the defendant.

"I will have order in this courtroom or I will clear it."

The judge's voice was respected.

"This is a teachable moment, and both attorneys should pay close attention. Too often, we parade people into this courtroom and courtrooms around the country who are not entirely aware of their rights. When we do that, we do a disservice not only to that client but to the justice system on the whole. I will not perpetrate that travesty in my courtroom. If I have to set aside a few minutes to ensure that a defendant is not only aware of their rights but able to execute them within the confines of the law, then I will do that. I am the judge. I can take that liberty. I have earned that right."

The courtroom was especially silent, and Judge Bledsoe's poignant words were heard clear.

"Now, Ms. Black, before you respond in haste, I am going to recess these proceedings for 30 minutes to give you an opportunity to speak with counsel and come to a decision as to how you want to proceed."

"I don't want him. It won't take me 30 minutes to decide that," Anna replied.

"I understand, but I am going to insist that you speak with Attorney Ross and see if the two of you can come to an understanding. We will reconvene in 30 minutes."

Judge Bledsoe leveled her gavel against the sound block, and court was temporarily adjourned. As soon as the judge retired to chambers and was no longer visible in the courtroom, there was a mad rush of reporters spilling out into the hallways and on the front steps of the courthouse. They wanted to be the first to report out on what was going on in the much anticipated Anna Black trial. Dr. Daniels and Detective Phillips took the opportunity to stretch their legs as well. The two of them exiting the courtroom made its own media splash as the bright lights of cameras were pointed in their direction. Reporters shoved microphones in their faces to get their reaction and to probe regarding other cases.

Instinctively, Michael placed one hand on the small of Chloe's back and used his other arm as a shield to protect her from the onslaught.

"Dr. Daniels, do you think this is a winnable case for the prosecution?"

"Dr. Daniels, what do you make of Anna Black's antics in the courtroom?"

"Was Judge Bledsoe too indulgent?" Is that grounds for a dismissal if pushed by either the prosecutor or the defense?"

"Was there a precedent set here? Will you be called on to testify?"

"Detective Phillips, will you be called to testify?"

More and more reporters fired an unending stream of questions at the duo. Michael spoke for both of them.

"No comment."

The cameras and personnel encircled the two until they reached the front steps of the courthouse. When the duo didn't stop and continued to walk near the edge of the grounds, only then did the last of the reporters who followed turn around and head back towards the building. They had a new target. Prosecutor Norwood had made her way to the courthouse steps. Dr. Daniels was glad for the distraction. No matter how many times it happened, it was always a little unnerving to have so many people bombarding her. Now that the two were alone, she could breathe a little easier. The sun was unseasonably bright, and the weather was pleasant; not too hot and not too cold.

"Thanks for the block back there," she offered.

"No problem," Michael replied with a smile. Chloe prepared to sit on one of the benches lining the court's walkway. Michael extended an arm to halt her downward movement.

"Hold up just a second."

Chloe straightened back up and watched as Michael dusted the spot where she was to sit.

"Now, that's better," he said as he dusted the place next to Chloe and joined her.

"Thanks," Chloe replied.

"You don't have to thank me, Dr. Daniels," Michael began. "That's what any man would do in my situation."

"And what situation is that?" Chloe asked teasingly.

"Looking out for you on all fronts," Michael answered without hesitation. That made Chloe blush, and she turned away from Michael as the heat rose in her cheeks. The old Michael would have let that moment pass, but this time he did not. Michael reached out and gently touched Chloe under the chin, turning her back in his direction. The rush of heat in her face rose higher, and Chloe dropped her gaze. Michael didn't let her go and didn't speak until she looked up and met his eyes. When he saw he had her, Michael smiled brilliantly, but his eyes remained soft and inviting.

"I will always look out for you."

Only then did he remove his hand. Chloe wanted to say thank you but had already been cautioned that thanks weren't necessary. Chloe acquiesced silently and smiled tentatively in response. The two fell silent. It was awkward for a moment. Then Michael lightened up the mood.

"It's kind of weird not having Addison around," he began. "Where is she?"

Chloe was grateful for the change of subject.

"She's at the office working on our other matter."

"The BD killer?"

"Yes, and gracias for not saying those words out loud."

The two laughed heartily. She liked that about Michael. There was an intensity that could be overwhelming but at the same time, there was a lightheartedness that offered great balance. Their light moment was abruptly interrupted.

"Dr. Daniels."

Chloe had to shield her eyes from the bright sun overhead to get a look at the person looming over her. The voice sounded eerily familiar, and when he stepped closer, his identity was confirmed.

"Nigel..."

Detective Phillips shifted on the bench as the man stepped closer.

"I was hoping to see you here," Nigel continued without acknowledgement of the person Chloe was in conversation with. She knew how Nigel operated and determined to set him straight without overt gesturing.

"Michael, this is Nigel. Nigel, this is Detective Michael Phillips."

Michael, being the gentleman that he was, stood to his feet and extended his hand.

"Good to meet you," he offered.

"And you as well, officer," Nigel replied firmly shaking Michael's hand.

"Detective," Chloe corrected. Nigel knew when he was being chastised and Chloe knew when Nigel was being a smart ass.

"Forgive me, detective," Nigel corrected, smirking.

Michael sat back down on the bench; this time a little closer to Chloe than he had been before.

"What brings you here, Nigel," Chloe asked, appreciating Michael's proximity.

"You requested my assistance, so I am here to oblige," Nigel beamed as he looked down at her. Remaining standing was all psychological play for him. Lauding over Chloe was authoritarian posturing. Had he chose to sit, it would have put him on the same level as the man currently sitting with her. Nigel always needed to distinguish himself. This situation was no different.

Chapter Two

Attorney Ross followed his client into the counseling room just down the hall from the courtroom. The guard ensured that the inmate was seated and her ankle chains securely attached to the chair before stepping away. The guard stood by while Ross conversed with his client. Ross didn't bother to sit down. Instead, he leaned against the wall across from inmate Black.

"What the hell were you thinking in there?"

Anna Black did not respond.

"I mean you embarrassed me! How dare you try to fire me?" Ross was incensed.

"I didn't try to fire you, sir, I did fire you," Anna replied pragmatically.

"That's what I hate about these free clients, no control, just absolutely ridiculous."

Attorney Ross was having a difficult time masking his true feelings. He was mumbling, but his client heard every word.

"Why are we in here?"

"What do you mean why are we in here? Didn't you hear Judge Bledsoe? She said you have to have a conversation with me before you fire me. It's not like I want to work your case anyway," Ross continued to fuss. "If I had a choice, trust me, Miss Black, I would be doing something else, but I was assigned to you. Therefore, I am responsible for what happens to you."

"I don't have anything to say to you, sir. I made myself very clear. You are fired."

"Do you understand, Miss Black that Prosecutor Norwood will have a field day with a new lawyer who has to bone up on this case? She is looking for a reason to make sure you are criminally prosecuted. I am fighting for you. I am fighting to get an insanity plea. That is the only way I can keep you out of jail. Do you understand that, Miss Black?"

"Yes, I understand your argument, but I am not crazy," Anna declared.

"Remember the conversation we had about you wanting to testify, Miss Black?"

"Yes and I still do."

"And remember when I told you how I didn't think that's such a good idea?"

"Yes, but that doesn't mean I don't have a right to defend myself and testifying is the way to do that."

"Do you understand that if you are found guilty of the charges that have been filed against you, you could get the death penalty, Miss Black?"

"That's why I need to testify Attorney Ross. I need to be able to explain to the judge, to the jury, and everybody else who's listening that I was helping those people. And no matter what you say, I am not crazy."

Attorney Ross was doing his best to be at least remotely professional, but Anna Black was such a frustrating client.

"So it sounds to me, Miss Black, like no matter what I say, your intention is to fire me. Is that correct?"

"That's correct."

"Okay then. Would you like for me to find another attorney from the public defender's office that would be willing to represent you?"

"How do I know if they are any better than you are?"

"I don't know, Miss Black, and I don't know what else to say. I don't know what else to do, and our time is up. I'll see you back in the courtroom."

"I think our 30-minute recess is just about over," Michael suggested. Chloe was grateful for the bailout.

"I think you're right," she replied. "Good to see you again, Nigel. I'm sure we'll talk soon."

Nigel was not to be so easily dismissed. He had every intention of making his presence known as he followed the duo back into the courtroom. Dr. Daniels heard his footsteps mimicking theirs, but she didn't bother to turn around. She remembered the games Nigel played in the past, and it looked to Chloe like he was still playing the same tired games. The doorway to the courtroom was crowded with people trying to regain their seats before the judge returned to the bench. Media personnel were pushing and shoving trying to make sure they had their seats and were privy to the continued drama they expected to unfold once court resumed.

The bailiff made the pronouncement that court was now in session. It was only after the courtroom quieted down did Judge Bledsoe return to the bench.

"Attorney Ross, has your client made a decision?"

"She has, your honor."

"Well, what is her decision?"

"I'm still fired, your honor."

There was muffled laughter from the gallery. Judge Bledsoe looked up. She didn't level her gavel this time, but the message was still very clear.

"Okay Miss Black, I understand you have fired public defender Ross is that correct?"

"Yes, your honor, judge."

"Ms. Black, please stand when addressing the court."

"I'm sorry, your most high honor," Anna offered as she stood to her feet.

"Yes, I did fire my attorney, and I am sticking with that decision."

"Would you want another attorney from the public defender's office appointed to your case?"

"I think I have another option, your honor ma'am."

"You do Miss Black, you do have another option," Judge Bledsoe replied, "and I will explain that option to you. But I want you to be very careful and think about whatever your decisions are going to be. Your freedom and your very life depend on the decisions you make right now. Do you understand that, Miss Black?"

"I fully understand, your honor. Don't I have the right to represent myself?"

"Yes, Miss Black you do. But there is a certain level of understanding of the law that is required when arguing a case in court."

"I may not have all the legal knowledge, your honor, I don't dispute that. But what I do have is the truth on my side. And I feel like, your honor, if I tell the truth, then this jury will understand that I have been merciful in all of my actions; that I have only desired to help people, that I have helped people cross over to a land that is much kinder than the one we know, your honor."

"I'm sorry, Miss Black," Judge Bledsoe interjected. "This is not the time to testify." Anna took her reprimand without responding. Anna's mother shook her head as if Anna could see her from behind. Carrie knew this wouldn't bode well for her child and she reached forward to intervene. Peter held her back. Carrie looked to him for answers. His eyes said what she didn't want to hear. Reluctantly, Carried resigned herself to her daughter's decision and slumped back in her seat.

"If self-representation is your decision, Ms. Black, then we will proceed with the case."

"That is my decision, your honor. I desire to represent myself."

"Understood," Judge Bledsoe advised. "Miss Black, please take your seat. Mr. Ross, you're hereby excused from the case. We will reconvene two days from today; that's Wednesday morning at 9 o'clock a.m. for opening statements. Miss Black, I hope you're ready. Court is adjourned."

Judge Bledsoe leveled the gavel and exited the courtroom. Once again the stampede was on. The news reporters had to inform the nation of Anna Black's decision. The guards moved to the defendant's table to escort Anna back to lock up. Anna took the opportunity to speak to her parents.

"I'm gonna make you so proud of me!"

Major had the gangster rap booming in the car as they made their way to the group home. The two were excited about what was next. So many people in that place had been so unnecessarily cruel to them; the idea of payback was enticing. It was like a high without the drugs.

Devereux Treatment Center was located in Kennesaw, Georgia, not far from Kennesaw State

University. The Center was located in an upscale neighborhood masked by large affluent homes and booming retail businesses. If you weren't looking for the residential center, you would miss it. Mimicking too much of the divide between the haves and the have not's, you could find the treatment center just on the other side of the railroad tracks.

Major maneuvered the car down the narrow path that led to the entrance. Devereux was a multi-building complex with rolling fields of grass, basketball and tennis courts; they even had a swimming pool. And all of it was encapsulated behind a twelve-foot barbed wire fence. Devereux is where they sent the bad kids. Devereux is where they sent the kids that could not be managed in a group home or a foster home. Devereux was one step short of jail. But to hear the social workers tell it, Devereux was about treatment, recovery, getting to the root of the problem; it wasn't incarceration, it was rehabilitation.

Major and Mayven knew that to be a flat-out lie. What the caseworkers didn't tell you was that once you entered Devereux, they stripped you of everything that identified you as an individual. They called it the probationary period. The time limit on probation was contingent on how well the new resident complied with the endless rules in learning the system.

Probation meant they took your real shoes and forced you to wear flip-flops; with socks when it was cold, to keep you from running away from the place. You were compelled to sleep in open air areas with no privacy. Probation meant you had to ask permission for everything; to go to the bathroom, to go outside, to talk on the telephone. Oh, you couldn't have your own phone. A personal cell phone could not be monitored. If you wanted to talk to somebody, you had to use Devereux's phone; the phone where they could hear everything you said on the other side. When you did go outside, you were required to walk in a straight line.

When you went to eat in the cafeteria, everybody ate the same thing. There was little to no regard for dietary restrictions based on religion or anything of the sort. And then they made you go to counseling. You had to sit there and tell a stranger about your problems. And if you refused to spill your deepest, darkest, most painful secrets, they coded you as noncompliant which meant your probationary period was extended until you did comply.

And school? Oh, you went to school, on campus. There were no outside activities once you were inside Devereux. It was only after you successfully navigated the reward system did you earn privileges like being able to walk on the grounds unaccompanied, inside the barbed-wire fence; or being able to have a conversation with another resident that wasn't monitored by an adult paid to be there to watch you. You could also earn the privilege of going off site. But that took a long time, and it had to be with somebody who had been vetted, not only by The Center but by your social worker and her supervisor and her supervisor's supervisor. And if you didn't have a relative who could make it all the way out to Kennesaw from Atlanta then the likelihood of you being able to go off site was slim to none. But this place was supposed to help you. That's what Major and Mayven resented the most; that the people entrusted to take care of them sent them to a place where they were treated like chattel.

As Major pulled up to the security guards' hut that sat just outside the twelve-foot tall black gate, he had to figure out the best way to maneuver in the situation. Fortunately, it was just a call box this time. It was during the day and the guard shack was empty of a real person. But they still had to pass mustard to gain access to the grounds. If Major gave their real names, he knew they wouldn't be able to get in. Major and Mayven ran from Devereux. There were runaway orders filed in juvenile court and with the police. The two would be welcomed back with handcuffs. That was not a viable option. If they said they were visiting with someone, the visitor's log would be checked against their names. That would be a problem. After turning the music down, Major pushed the button. The sound box cracked and a perky voice on the other end addressed the visitor.

"Welcome to Devereux! How may I help you?"

Mayven rolled her eyes. Major popped his lips.

"We're here to see one of the counselors."

"And have you been here before?"

"Yes, ma'am we have."

"And who is it that you want to see?"

Major paused briefly trying to remember. Mayven leaned over and gave him a name.

"We are here to see counselor Thornton."

The sound box went silent.

"Good looking out May," Major said to his girl. She smiled in response.

"Okay, Ms. Thornton? Let me just check. Hold on one second please."

Again there was silence on the other end. Major and Mayven didn't know if this would work, but they were definitely willing to give it a try. What they knew is that counselors often saw family members and other private parties from outside Devereux as a way to supplement the income the facility made. So it wouldn't be uncommon for someone coming on campus just to see one of them. When the call box cracked again, the receptionist replied.

"Okay, I'm going to buzz the gate. Wait until it slides all the way back before attempting to enter. Thank you." The two thought they were home free and then the voice on the other end had something else to say.

And make sure you stop at the visitor's center to get your identification badges before going back to the counselor."

"Will do," Major lied. The two had no intention of going anywhere near the visitors' center.

Major and Mayven weren't out of the woods yet. They had to successfully negotiate their way to the designated location without intervention from any Devereux staff. The benefit of having lived there for more than 18 months, Major and Maven knew the blind spots on campus, and they also knew staff didn't have weapons. Staff had no real way of protecting themselves. What they did have was scare tactics, walkie-talkies, and numbers; only because the residents never rallied together to overtake them. Major and Mayven still had friends locked up behind the walls of Deveraux.

And they knew that if they got to their friends first, they could increase their numbers and take down those staff persons who had treated them so poorly in the past. It would have been easy just to make a phone call, plan and plot the whole thing out with those who still lived behind the wall. But those folks never made it on the behavioral chart to earn privileges to get any personal phone calls. Major and Mayven had to make direct contact by being on campus. All they needed was a distraction. They could handle the rest.

Chapter Three

"Who is Michael?"

"What?"

Lynette did her best not to get upset. She asked the question again.

"Fatima, who is Michael?"

"Come on now Lyn, you know I don't have time for this. I'm already running late for work."

"Who is Michael, Fatima? You were moaning and groaning and grinding on me calling out the name of someone else. A fuckin' man. So who is Michael, Fatima?"

Fatima continued to try and avoid the question. She didn't want to have to answer because to answer meant she would break Lynette's, heart.

"I am not going to stop asking and you're going to answer me. I deserve that, Fatima. I deserve an answer, so answer me dammit! Who the fuck is Michael?"

Fatima did the only thing she knew to do. Instead of trying to avoid Lynette, she walked up to her, extending and then wrapping her arms around Lynette even though her lover resisted.

"It doesn't matter who Michael is, Lyn," Fatima whispered in her ear.

"I love you, girl. I come home every night to you. Don't you know how much I care about you?"

Lynette squirmed to get away. She fought hard enough to get out of Fatima's clutches.

"Don't Fatima. I'm not one of those little girls you used to secretly fuck back in the day when you were still undecided about who you were. I'm a grown-ass woman, and I know what I heard. So once again, who the fuck is Michael?"

Lynette wasn't trying to hear it today.

"And when you get through with that smooth-talking bullshit, the question is still the same. Who the fuck is Michael?"

Fatima knew Lynette would persist. She knew Lyn wouldn't be able to just let this go, but she had to try. To confess to who Michael really was would certainly drive a wedge between the two of them that would never be able to be removed. That's why Fatima had to lie. She had to try to cover it up.

"Listen, Lynette; I was sleeping. You can't hold me accountable for some shit I said when I was sleep."

"Is that how you gone try to play me, Fatima, like I'm dumb?"

"I didn't say that," Fatima defended. "Come on now, babe. You know I wouldn't do nothing like that to you."

"But you do think I'm dumb, don't you? You have to Fatima. You didn't just call his name one time, you called his name over and over. And when I was finger fuckin' you, you screamed out his name, not mine. His name, Fatima! Now, maybe I could look over it, get past it, act like you didn't say it if you at least called another bitches name. But you called his name. So who the fuck is Michael?"

Fatima felt defeated as she sat down on the edge of their bed. She dropped her head. She didn't know what to say. Lynette sat down next to her. She was still fuming and refused to allow the love of her life to get off easy. Lynn dedicated the last few years of her life to Fatima, and she deserved an answer. Lynette was determined to get that answer.

"I'm going to ask you one more time, Fatima, and you think long and hard before you consider lying to me or faking like you didn't say what you said," Lynette clarified. "Who is Michael?"

With Lynette sitting in such close proximity to her, Fatima could feel the waves of intense energy emerging for her person. That once magnetic, sexual attraction had been replaced with tension and pain tinged anxiety. Fatima knew she had to answer. She owed Lynette that much.

"He's a police officer," Fatima mumbled.

"I'm listening, Fatima. There has to be more to it than that, so start talking before I start walking; because I am fully prepared to pack my things and leave our home if you don't get honest with me real quick," Lynette insisted.

"Okay, okay, Lynette. He's a police officer from Atlanta. He came into town to help with a case I'm working on."

Fatima knew her response wasn't sufficient, especially after Lynette put her hand on her hip and gave her that look. Fatima didn't make eye contact with her lover as she tried to explain.

"I don't know... it was something about him that I found attractive. And apparently, it spilled over into my dreams, Lynette. Damn, I don't know what else to say."

Lynette wanted to know the truth, but the truth was painful. She sat there quietly trying to make sense of what her lover just said. For Fatima to be attracted to a man to the point that it infiltrated her dreams was very concerning to Lynette. Lyn

34

was a lesbian. She loved women. The thought of being intimate with a man repulsed Lynette to a certain degree. And for her lover to be fantasizing and getting off on the thought of a man she barely knew said a whole lot to Lynette. She didn't know what to say. Lynette fought back the urge to cry and scream.

"It's interesting, Fatima," Lynette began. "In all that explaining you just did, you never once said his name. Not once…"

The ability to suppress what was brewing just beneath the surface became increasingly difficult. Lynette could feel her stomach knotting and her heart rate surging.

"Do you want him?"

"What?"

"Fatima, do you want this Michael person? Do you want him?" Lynette's voice cracked as she emphasized every syllable of every word.

Even as she asked, Lynette regretted the question. What if she got an answer she wasn't prepared to receive? The fact that Fatima hesitated before answering; restating the question to buy herself time to formulate an answer, was really answer enough. And even with space and time to vehemently deny it, Fatima sat quietly, wrestling with her own demons. That was all the confirmation Lynette needed.

Slowly, Lynette got up from the bed, walked to the closet, opened the door, and found a bag. As tears streamed down her cheeks, Lynette grabbed whatever she could find that belonged to her and started shoving it into the duffle. Her cries became louder. Fatima went to her.

"Awe babe, come on now. You know I love you. I don't want him, I want you."

Without hesitation, Lynette lashed out and slapped Fatima with an open hand.

"You're lying! You're lying to me, to my face, Fatima! You're lying!"

Every word was enunciated by Lynette throwing her feelings with her fists. Fatima blocked the blows. She knew in her heart Lynette wasn't trying to hurt her. Lynette was hurt and striking out to express the pain Fatima caused. When Lynette cried out and crumpled to the floor, Fatima met her there and consoled her.

"I'm so sorry, Lynn," Fatima offered. "I'm so sorry. I didn't mean to hurt you."

"But you did Fatima, you did hurt me."

"It was just a dream, Lynn," Fatima explained. "I have never done anything with this man. I don't want him. I want you."

Lynette looked up with sorrow-filled eyes.

"I wish I could say I believe you."

Tanner Jr. was having an increasingly difficult time trying to manage his emotions. He desperately wanted to find his sister, but everything he and his dad tried so far came up empty. Tanner Sr. could see the dejection on his son's face.

"What are we going to do now, dad? She's not here. Where could she be?"

Tanner Sr. wished he had an answer for his son. He was starting to feel the same kind of desperation. But as the father, Tanner Sr. had to be strong.

"I don't know what we're supposed to do next, son. Give me a minute. I need a minute to think about it."

The two walked slowly back to their vehicle. Tanner Sr. unlocked the doors, and both of them climbed in. Tanner Sr. left the car keys on top of the dashboard. Start the car? Where would they go? He really didn't know what the next best move would be. So they sat there; the two of them in silence. He never wanted to think the worst about this situation, but things weren't looking so good at the moment. Maybe he should call the hospitals to see if Tangela had been in an accident? Thinking that his daughter could be all alone, somewhere hurt made Tanner Sr. feel unwell himself.

The early morning fog was unusually thick. The sky was still relatively dark. The midnight glow of the moon had not yet been replaced by the rising sun that remained hidden from view. But he knew this road well, even in the faint light, he knew the straight ways, the hills, and the curves. He could barely see a few feet in front of him. Nevertheless, Logan Spencer pressed forward, putting one foot in front of the other as he executed his morning jog. Logan focused on his breathing; deep breaths in, deep breaths out. He didn't concentrate on the familiar burning in his calves. Logan didn't regard the infrequent jogger moving passed him. He didn't think about how far he had come or how far he still had to go. Here is where Logan excised the demons from his past. Here is where he remembered.

Chapter Four

With her latest plans unceremoniously foiled by her insolent husband, Grace was beside herself. And then to top it off, hearing from the tow company about that other girls' car did not make her happy. Grace still hadn't figured out what, if anything, she needed to do about that. If she paid the bill with a credit card, the car could then be traced back to her, if someone thought enough to look. So for now, Grace decided to do nothing. What was the worst that could happen? Right now, though, she had to get her own vehicle. She needed it because there would be another kill.

Grace thought about having Drake take her to the mechanic to pick up her van but at the moment, Grace couldn't stand the sight of him. Grace did something she hadn't done in a while. She phoned a friend.

"Priscilla?"

"Grace Pembroke Wetherby, to what do I owe this long overdue pleasure?"

Priscilla Patton Middleton was a socialite and very influential in the arts community. Endowments were named after her family. That's why Grace was her 'friend'.

"Now Priscilla," Grace began, faking endearment the entire time. "Don't hold it against me. Last I heard you were out of the country. I was just waiting to hear all about your latest escapades."

"Brussels was fantastic," Priscilla oozed. "We definitely need to catch up. I'm sure you've been busy since I was away?"

If she only knew, Grace thought.

"I'm sure nothing as fabulous as your time in Brussels."

"We should catch up," Priscilla suggested. "Let's say tea, next week?"

"Actually Priscilla, I need a favor today."

Priscilla paused. This was not how things were done in their circle.

"And what is that, dear?"

This was not proper social etiquette, but Priscilla was intrigued by what Grace could have possibly needed from her.

"I had a flat tire the other night. It was a horrific experience," Grace began, attempting to play to Priscilla's sympathy.

"So sorry to hear that, dear," Priscilla added as Grace continued.

"And that's why I need you," Grace continued. "My vehicle is ready, and I need a lift."

"Drake should see to that, don't you think," Priscilla asked snidely. Grace knew Priscilla was all about traditional appearances; men handling men's things, blah, blah, blah.

"Ordinarily he would, Priscilla," Grace defended. "But he's tied up handling a business matter, and I don't want to pull him away from it. You understand."

"I do," Priscilla chimed. "Business must be handled."

"So you see why I need my oldest and dearest friend to assist me with this?"

Grace heard Priscilla sigh on the other end. She was too snobbish to mask it.

"This won't take long, promise," Grace added in for good measure.

There was another discernable pause before Priscilla responded.

"Fine, Grace, but this can't take too long. I have a nail appointment early evening that I can't afford to miss."

"All I need you to do is pick me up and drop me off. That shouldn't be long at all. Be here in 15?"

"I'll be there shortly."

Priscilla ended the call. Grace didn't care that Priscilla was not enthusiastic about helping her. People in her group of friends used each other for their own benefit all the time. It was nothing new.

Fortunately, Priscilla prided herself on being timely and arrived at the Wetherby home on schedule. Grace didn't wait for her to get out of the car. Instead, she was coming out as Priscilla tooted the horn on her Audi station wagon.

"Thanks so much for fitting me into your busy schedule, Priscilla," Grace quipped as she sat down in the passenger's seat.

"No problem, Grace, how've you been?"

"Just lovely," Grace commented.

"Which direction should we go?"

Grace gave Priscilla the address which she promptly put into her GPS. Priscilla talked about her trip and herself the entire car ride. Grace tuned out as much of it as she could.

"Grace, Grace are you listening," Priscilla asked slightly irritated by the thought of being ignored.

"I'm sorry Priscilla, what were you blabbering on about?"

Priscilla slammed hard on the brakes at the stop sign.

"Must you be so petulant?" Priscilla screeched. "Remember Missy, I'm doing you a favor."

Grace struggled to maintain the façade between who she was and who she pretended to be all these years. But once again, the lack of filter on her thoughts and what subsequently spewed from her lips wasn't serving her well.

"Forgive me, Priscilla," Grace began, attempting to sound sincere. "It's just..."

Now she had Priscilla's full attention to the point that the car behind them blew the horn to get them to move. Priscilla waved a polite hand as she entered the intersection. Grace cursed at them.

"Fuckers..."

"Grace Wetherby!" Priscilla chastised. That kind of vernacular was not appreciated in polite society. "What in the world has gotten into you?"

Grace attempted to look sorry for her outburst. She counted a few beats for dramatic effect before responding.

"Priscilla, I can't talk about it," she sighed.

"Now Grace, you and I have been friends a long time," Priscilla began. "You know you can trust me." Grace noticed that Priscilla slowed the car down. The longer it took to arrive at their destination, the more time Grace had to spill her guts; fodder for the next meeting of the socialite club.

Nosey bitch, Grace thought as she decided to play along. Feigning tears, Grace continued.

"Promise you won't speak a word of this to anyone."

"I promise, Grace."

Lying bitch...

"...it's Drake..."

"Oh no, Grace, honey, do tell." Grace could hear the eagerness in Priscilla's voice.

"I think he's going to leave me," Grace gasped.

Priscilla clutched at her imaginary pearls.

"Whatever for?"

"You know how it can be after you've been married as long as we have. You get comfortable with each other, don't work as hard..."

They were nearing the mechanic's shop.

"I completely understand," Priscilla advised. "You don't think..."

Priscilla allowed her voice to drop off.

"I do think," Grace replied, sounding heartbroken.

"Grace, no!"

"I can't talk about it anymore," Grace surmised.

Priscilla pulled the car into the shop's lot and put the car in park. When she reached to turn off the ignition, Grace tried to stop her.

"Thanks, Priscilla, you don't have to stay," Grace suggested.

"What are friends for," Priscilla asked, proceeding to turn off the ignition and grab her purse from the back seat.

"Really, you don't have to," Grace advised, moving quickly to get out of the passenger door.

"With your fragile condition and everything that's going on, it's the least I can do. Besides, what if they messed something up? You'll need a ride home."

Priscilla was out of the car before Grace could protest any further. Not having much choice, Grace intended to make the transaction as quick as possible so she could rid herself of her 'friend'. Priscilla fulfilled her usefulness, and now Grace didn't need or want her around anymore.

The two crossed the lot, tiptoeing to avoid holes and pitfalls along the way. The door to the shop looked greasy. Priscilla stepped in, grabbing a kerchief from her purse and handing it to Grace so she could open the door. The inside of the shop smelled thick with grease and oil. It was enough to turn the prudish ladies' stomachs. Priscilla put a polite finger to her nose while Grace used the kerchief to ring the bell on the stained desk. After a few minutes, someone came from the back of the shop.

"May I help you?"

"I'm Mrs. Wetherby."

Raoul remembered this one from the phone call earlier. He decided as long as she was polite, he would remain professional.

"Your van is ready. The total is $236.00. How do you want to pay?"

Grace reached into her purse and pulled out her Black American Express card. Instead of placing the card in Raoul's outstretched hand, Grace took the kerchief and sat the card on the counter.

Raoul looked at the card and then looked up at her. He decided to hold his peace and get the bitch out of his shop as quickly as possible. He swiped the card and placed the card, receipt for signature and a pen on the counter. Grace picked up the pen in her covered hand and scribbled her name. She retrieved her belongings without touching them with her naked hand.

"If you will wait out front, I'll pull the van around."

"It should have been already out there. You knew I was coming," Grace snipped. Raoul didn't acknowledge her and disappeared into the back of the shop. As the ladies exited, Grace gave Priscilla another opportunity to leave.

"Thanks again, Priscilla, dear," Grace began. "Everything has been handled. I don't want you to miss your appointment."

"You're almost done. Let's just get you in the van and then I will know everything is okay." Priscilla would not be dismissed so easily. Besides, she wanted to hear more of Grace's tragic situation.

They waited for the van to be pulled around and when it was, Grace was relieved to see that the tire had been replaced. Raoul exited the van.

"Before you pull off, I just wanted to point something out to you."

Raoul walked to the passenger side of the van and released the lock on the sliding door. Priscilla and Grace followed. When Grace saw where the mechanic stopped, her heart dropped. Had she left something for someone to find?

"When we were working on your vehicle, we found this large staining in the carpet. I wanted to bring it to your attention. I didn't want you to get home and see it and think we did it. The staining was there when we picked up the van."

Grace was mortified. She knew exactly what the dark staining was. Before she could respond, Priscilla leaned into the vehicle to take a closer look. Grace's heart skipped a beat.

"Grace," Priscilla began. "What is that? It looks like..."

Grace interrupted before Priscilla could finish her thought.

"You should have said something about this when you called me earlier. How do I know one of your mechanics didn't do it?"

"Ma'am I would have told you had you given me a chance when we spoke earlier, but you were so focused on the time issue, and then hung up on me, I didn't get a chance."

"Fine, whatever, as long as my van is repaired." Grace was quick to hit the button to get the door to close.

"Grace what is that?" Priscilla wasn't willing to let it go that quickly. The red tinge to the stain concerned her.

"It's nothing, Priscilla, now can we just go?" Grace was growing impatient.

"I've got my car back, thanks for the ride, I'll see you later," Grace called over her shoulder as she made her way around the back of the van to the driver's seat. Priscilla was still trying to get Grace's attention as Grace put the van in reverse and started to back out.

"Grace! Grace I know you hear me!"

Grace waved to Priscilla and mouthed thank you as she put the van in drive and pulled off.

"That bitch," Priscilla screeched as she placed her hand on her thin hip.

"Maybe that's why Drake is leaving you..." Priscilla hissed as she made her way to her own car. She wouldn't so easily let Grace get away with being rude. Priscilla had no intention of letting this one go.

Chapter Five

Major drove the car to an obscure location on campus, minding the high-speed bumps that shook the car every time they crossed one. There were several outbuildings on the edge of campus and Major pulled the car into a parking space behind one of them. After the car was parked, Major and Mayven got out. With a quick double check of their personal weapons, Major went to the trunk to get the kill kit.

"Can't forget this," he said to Mayven, as he rounded the car from the rear.

Being mindful of their surroundings and checking for adults wandering the campus, Major and Mayven began walking on foot toward the resident houses. The schedule at Devereux never changed, and they knew the residents would soon be leaving out, building by building to return from classes before dinner. On foot, Major and Mayven would be able to blend in with the rest of the residents walking across campus.

The twosome laid low, staying close to one of the outer buildings.

"You ready for this May," Major asked as they crouched close together.

"With you, I'm always ready," she replied smiling.

Mayven gave Major a quick peck on the cheek. Major smiled widely. He loved her affection. It made him feel strong, extra confident. It didn't take long before there was movement on the campus. Just like clockwork, activity increased as residents moved from their classrooms and therapy sessions towards the individual cottages. That's when they moved, coming out of hiding and falling in line with the other kids. It would be difficult for staff to differentiate the twosome from the other residents because there were just so many bodies moving at once. The staff to resident ratio was never what it was supposed to be. The staff at Devereux didn't tend to last too long, and the turnover rate was exceptionally high. Dealing with kids with behavioral disorders, psychiatric diagnoses, and bad attitudes tended to wear a person out in a short period of time. That worked to Major and Mayven's advantage. They blended in virtually undetected.

The residents they walked with certainly noticed the two new kids. There was a slight buzz of 'who is that' and 'where did they come from' but nothing to alert the staff who were following at the back of the group. Major and Mayven kept their eyes peeled for the familiar; someone they knew in one of their old houses. Mayven was the first to recognize someone they both knew. She moved through the crowd, made her way over to her, and fell in step with her old friend. Belinda Carlisle, or as her friends called her, Pinky, didn't pay attention at first. She was focused on getting where she was going and someone falling in next to her wasn't worthy of a response, as long as they didn't touch her. But that's exactly what Mayven did; nudging Pinky just a little; just enough to get her attention but not enough to piss her off. Everybody knew Pinky had a short fuse and would strike first and ask questions later.

"What the..." Pinky uttered; her fists immediately balling up, ready to correct whoever got too close.

"Wassup girl," Mayven said quickly, making sure to make eye contact with Pinky. Only when Belinda stepped back a second and recognized who it was did her fists relax.

"What the fuck you doing back up in this bitch?"

Pinky was glad to see Mayven. She didn't allow herself to get close to too many people, but she and Mayven became fast friends.

"Cool out," Mayven whispered. "Me and Major both here," Mayven continued. "It's some folks we need to take care of."

Mayven checked in with Pinky to see if she understood what it was Mayven was and wasn't saying. There were a lot of kids around that neither of them knew. Mayven didn't want one of them overhearing and ratting them out to staff. But Pinky did catch on and started to smile.

"Straight up?"

"Straight up," Mayven confirmed. "You down?"

"Hell yeah," Pinky chimed in. "Long as I get to get me some, too," she exclaimed, knocking her fists together.

"Cool," Mayven replied, shushing Pinky once again. "Back door, your house, ten minutes, alright?"

Pinky nodded her understanding and the two friends momentarily parted ways. Mayven weaved her way back to where Major was walking to alert him to what was going on. As the crowd started to disperse, each group heading toward their houses, Major and Mayven were very careful to stay in the middle of the pack. Staff would be aligning with their groups and the closer they got to their respective places, the more staff would likely be paying attention. Major was especially careful to keep the duffle bag in front of him, away from the eyes of staff who may be scanning the group.

The resident houses sat near the back of campus with enough distance between them so there was a semblance of privacy. There was a large communal field immediately in front of the cottages and a walking track that traveled behind and around them. Most of the residents cut through the field to get to their destination. Major and Mayven made sure to stay close to the group and only trail off at the last minute; ducking between two buildings. Prater House was their destination, and the twosome stayed low and close as they worked towards Mayven's old stomping ground. Some of the staff in her building had been cool, but there were others who used the residents like tools; treating them less than human for their own amusement.

Pinky walked into Prater House as she normally did. There were 12 residents in the house. The other 11 knew to move out of Pinky's way when she came through. Some thought Pinky was a bully. Pinky described herself as misunderstood. Either way, nobody, even staff, got in her way. There were two staff members on duty. Monica

Jiles was relatively new to Devereux. She worked in child welfare before but had only been with Devereux for about six months. Carmelita Woolfolk, the other staff person on duty, was an old head. She'd been with the agency for years. Carmelita was still working resident level even though she felt she had the skills necessary to move up. As she was the last one into the cottage, Carmelita pulled out the ring of keys and locked the front door.

It was getting close to the time when Pinky should be opening the back door. Major was pumped. Any time they were doing clandestine work with a surprise element? That always hyped him up. Mayven was ready, too. The butterflies in her stomach didn't make her nervous. It was a familiar feeling Mayven grew to expect. It just reminded her to be alert and on her P's and Q's when it was time to move. Just like there was a schedule outside of the houses, there was a schedule once the residents were 'home'. If the schedule stayed true to form, all the residents would be in the common areas doing homework, or something else staff deemed constructive. Residents were not allowed to go to their bedrooms until immediately before bedtime. Mayven was counting on the schedule staying the same.

Carmelita and Monica were positioned in the staff office right alongside the common area.

"I need to go to the bathroom," Pinky announced from commons.

"Go head," Monica called out without looking up. Carmelita barely paid attention as she busied herself playing games on her cell phone.

Pinky exited commons and headed toward the bathroom on the main hall. Once out of eyesight, she took a slight detour and moved to the back of the cottage. There was an alert on the back door. It would chime throughout the cottage but not outside the house. Major and Mayven would have to be quick upon entrance so the door could be closed quickly and the chime silenced.

Pinky pushed the door open. The chime sounded. Mayven and Major slipped in.

"What's going on," Carmelita called out from the office; getting up out of her chair and moving toward the alarm.

"These damn kids," Carmelita muttered under her breath as she stomped down the hallway to investigate. She didn't see it coming, only felt the blow as Pinky stepped out from a doorway and cold cocked her. Carmelita stumbled; grabbing the side of her head where she'd been punched. Before she could fully recover, Pinky was on top of her, slamming her fist into Carmelita's face unrelentingly.

"I ain't never liked you no way, bitch," Pinky grumbled as she beat Carmelita nearly unconscious. All the staff person could do was try and cover her head. Pinky outweighed her by almost 50 pounds and had her at a decided disadvantage. Carmelita protested, but her murmurs were quickly covered up by the sounds coming from the common areas. The residents lived for a break in the rules; just like inmates in prison, any disturbance allowed them the opportunity to break even more rules.

With Carmelita being handled, Major and Mayven made their way to the office. Monica heard the disturbance outside the office and got to her feet to see what was going on. The residents hooped and hollered as the twosome crossed the commons toward the office. Monica saw a man moving in her direction. She momentarily froze. That was just enough time for Major to sprint toward her catching her with a forearm to the neck and knocking her backward. Monica hit her head hard against the chair as she fell to the ground. She was dazed. Mayven moved in, adding a few unexpected blows to the face. Some of the residents crowded around the office door, screaming their approval.

"Get that hoe!"

"Beat that ass!"

"Get the fuck out the way," Pinky's voice boomed as she moved toward the office, dragging Carmelita by the ponytail. As Pinky turned the corner around the dining table, Carmelita's ponytail came off in her hand.

"...da fuck?"

Pinky held the detached hair high over her head. A few of the residents cackled with laughter at Carmelita's embarrassment. She was nearly unconscious from the beating she took and could barely respond.

"Who wants this raggedy shit?" Pinky asked; waving the hair around.

"Me! Me!" A few of the residents called out.

Pinky put the hair to her nose and sniffed.

"It's stanky as hell but y'all can have it!"

Pinky whirled the ponytail around and tossed it toward the residents who were vying for it. The residents at the table scrambled for it, and two ended up tussling over it.

"Give it to me! It's mine trick, let it go!"

Carmelita started to come to. Pinky felt movement as she moved to adjust her grip. She could no longer hold Carmelita by the hair, so instead, Pinky grabbed the staffer's shirt collar and choked her up. When she felt a bit of resistance, Pinky swung her leg hard; connecting with the small of Carmelita's back.

"Be still dammit!"

Carmelita moaned in pain as Pinky proceeded to drag her the rest of the way to the office. Major and Mayven had been busy. Major picked Monica up off the floor while Mayven righted the chair that had been knocked over. Major plopped the wounded staff person in the chair, and Mayven got to work with the kill kit. She pulled out the duct tape and began wrapping it around Monica, binding her to the chair.

"I brought you a present," Pinky announced as she dragged Carmelita into the office.

"Nice work," Major congratulated; making room for the two new entrants.

"That's who I want," Mayven announced when she saw Carmelita. Major took over, making sure Monica was secured in the chair.

Mayven abandoned her work with Monica and met Carmelita where she lay. Mayven straddled the ailing worker and promptly backhanded her several times as Pinky continued to hold her in place. Blood spewed from Carmelita's lips; flying in all directions. The sting to Carmelita's face woke her from her haze. It took a minute for her eyes to focus. Mayven waited patiently as Carmelita blinked several times, trying to clear the cobwebs.

"Wakey, wakey, bitch," Mayven encouraged with another solid backhand to Carmelita's face. Instinctively, Carmelita reached up toward her face to address the newest sting. Mayven smacked her hand out of the way and slapped her again for good measure.

"Bitch slap that hoe again, May," Pinky encouraged.

Mayven responded, slapping Carmelita once again.

"...stop..." Carmelita whined as the words she intended to speak finally found their way to her bloody mouth.

"What?" Mayven questioned. "What did you say?"

"...please...stop..." Carmelita whispered, wincing through bleeding lips.

"Did that bitch say please," Major asked from across the room.

"Yeah, she did Maj," Mayven replied. "Begging and shit now, but what about when it was reversed?" Mayven questioned Carmelita; snatching her up by the chin and forcing Carmelita to look at her.

Recognition slowly set in as Carmelita was made to focus her eyes. With recognition came flashes of memory and Carmelita's eyes swelled in their sockets.

"Yeah bitch, it's me."

Mayven moved in even closer, ensuring Carmelita was unable to look away. She wanted her oppressor to take a good hard look at her before Mayven shut her eyes; maybe permanently.

Carmelita started to blubber as their collective past registered firmly in her mind. This was payback, and Carmelita knew it.

"That hoe crying already," Pinky chimed in. She had her own score to settle with Carmelita. She used her authority in the house as personal power; demeaning the residents every chance she got. Now, it was time for reconciliation.

"...you ... won't...get ... away... with ... this," Carmelita warned, even in her compromised position.

"This damn fool still trying to threaten some damn body! What the fuck is wrong with her?" Mayven questioned to no one in particular.

"Get away with what," Mayven asked, hawking and then spitting in Carmelita's face. Carmelita tried to close her eyes as she saw the spittle coming but she was too slow, and Mayven's venom hit her squarely in the eye.

"Ugghhhh," she cried out.

"Let me help you with that, Ms. Lita," Pinky chimed in; using her free hand to grab the end of her shirt. Leaning over, Pinky smeared Mayven's leavings all over Carmelita's face.

"There, that's better," Pinky said with a smile.

"Thank you, girl," Mayven added. "Now get that hoe in the chair."

Pinky was more than happy to oblige. She lifted Carmelita with both hands and dragged her to the empty office chair. Major finished securing Monica and waited for Carmelita to be positioned.

"I want in on this shit! Them bitches been fuckin with me since I got here," one of the residents announced as she tried to make her way into the office.

"You'll get your chance, I promise," Major advised as he gently pushed her back out of the office. "Er'body will get they chance, a'ight?"

The remaining girl's cheered hearing Major's promise. They all had individual vendettas and scores to settle. The group looked on eagerly waiting for their chance to jump in.

Pinky helped Mayven tape Carmelita in the chair. Monica, who was slowly coming to, began to realize their joint plight.

"Please, don't do this," she begged. "I haven't done anything."

"Sorry, baby girl," Major replied. "Wrong place, wrong time... shit happens."

"They all alike any damn way," Pinky chimed in. "Making folks life miserable and shit. Fuck that bitch, too."

Major laughed. He understood what Pinky was talking about. Once the girls had Carmelita strapped down in the chair, both Pinky and Mayven stepped back.

"Major, baby, what do you think we should do with these ladies?" Mayven asked, reaching for her knife securely held in her sheath.

"Well May," he began, pulling his pistol from his waistband, "looks like we got some help with this one."

Mayven released her blade and passed it in front of their victims. Each responded similarly with enlarged eyes and murmurs on their lips.

"Don't say shit," Mayven scolded. "He didn't ask you!"

Monica obeyed the command, but Carmelita wasn't so quick to follow along.

"Help me," she stuttered. "Help me," Carmelita repeated; her eyes shooting passed Mayven toward the doorway.

"I don't think they heard you," Mayven responded. "Hold on a sec."

Mayven walked toward the entrance to the office.

"That bitch Carmelita is asking for help. Anyone of y'all wanna help a hoe?"

Some of the girls laughed.

"I'll help that, trick," one of the girls chimed in. "Help y'all beat the shit out of her."

The group erupted again. A few of the girls gave high fives as they agreed with the response.

"I can't wait," one girl replied.

"You ain't by yo 'self," another girl chimed in.

Mayven focused her attention back on Carmelita as she crossed the office, wielding the blade in her hand.

"Don't look like nobody want to help you, Ms. Woolfolk," Mayven sneered.

Worry lines etched Carmelita's swelling face. They were matched by the concern written all over Monica's.

Carmelita looked from one to the other to see if either of them would be reasonable. Her lip hurt and every time she tried to speak, the healed over areas would reopen, and fresh blood would spill from her mouth.

"Belinda, please," she uttered; her eyes begging for mercy from what already happened and what she anticipated would happen next.

Belinda looked at her astonished.

"I know you ain't asking me," Pinky giggled.

"Belinda, please," Monica added, looking equally pensive.

Pinky looked at each of the women and sized them up.

"Ain't neither one of y'all ever done nothing for me, nothing. So why the fuck would I help you? Especially you Lita," Pinky continued. "You mean and shit... mean for no reason."

Pinky moved closer to Carmelita who reared back as the young lady approached. Pinky invaded Carmelita's personal space, imposing her size and demeanor on her.

"I wouldn't help yo sorry ass if God himself told me I had to, to make it into heaven." Pinky contended. She chuckled and then leaned down closer to Carmelita to make sure she could hear her.

"Im'ma bust hell wide open, and I'll see yo bitch ass there."

"I guess that's another no for you, Ms. Woolfolk," Mayven teased.

"Damn straight," Major added.

Pinky raised her hand as if to strike Carmelita. In anticipation, Carmelita closed her eyes and jerked away so hard that she lifted the chair from the floor. It balanced on two legs for the slightest second. Seeing the chair tilting, Pinky decided to give it a kick and help the chair over. Carmelita went spilling onto the floor as the chair crashed down with her in it.

"Oops," Pinky exclaimed. She walked over the chair, not giving Carmelita a second thought.

Mayven continued to twirl the tip of the blade in her fingers.

"I was thinking Major," she began, looking to her lover with a spark in her eye. "We could let the girls have these two and go to your old stomp to handle the rest of our business."

Major rubbed the barrel of the gun against the stubble on his chin.

"That's cool, I'm with that, but I don't like to leave witnesses," Major added.

"True, true," Mayven agreed. "But I dunno if we have to worry too much about either of these hoes talking."

"Why you think that, May?"

"Cause Pinky gone make sure to beat the black off they asses."

Pinky nodded her head in agreement.

"May, you know I gotcha girl. Ain't neither one of these skanks gone be saying shit."

"That's wassup, Pinky," Major said.

"But before we go, boo, I need to give Ms. Woolfolk something to remember me by," Mayven added.

"Do that shit, May," Major encouraged.

Pinky moved without asking, and Major followed suit, righting Carmelita's chair back up to a sitting position.

A knot was just forming on her head from the fall. She was in a lot of pain, and the tears brimming on her lids said so.

"Your tears do not move me, Carmelita, not one bit. I cried out to you plenty of times when I lived here. And you acted like you cared, but you really didn't. You remember when you told me I could tell you anything? That whatever I said was confidential and I could trust you? You remember that shit, Carmelita? And I believed you like a damn fool; thinking you really cared about me 'cause you said you did. You told me you cared about what happened to me, that you wanted the best for me, that you were here to help me. You remember that shit, Carmelita?"

Ms. Woolfolk did remember. She remembered the late night conversations when Mayven would have a nightmare, and she would go in to see about her. Carmelita remembered how Mayven learned to trust her over time; coming out of her shell and letting Carmelita know some of the things that happened to her in the past. Carmelita remembered all of that as tears began to stream down her cheeks.

"I asked you a question bitch! I know you heard me!"

Mayven's cold exterior began to crack as she too remembered. Taking the blunt end of her knife, Mayven came down hard across Carmelita's cheek, jarring several of her teeth loose from the strike. A stream of crimson red blood poured from Carmelita's mouth. Pinky got a kick out of it, and there were oohs and aahs from the girls looking on.

Carmelita struggled to answer. Her mouth hurt so bad; the bitter taste of her own blood slathered her tongue.

Mayven wasn't satisfied. She grabbed Carmelita by the hair and nodded her head for her.

"When I ask a question, the least you could do is answer me, shit..."

"You see these girls in here? You know why they want to get at yo' ass so bad? It's probably because you did the same thing to them like you did to me." Mayven held the hairs of Carmelita's head tightly in her hand as she continued.

"You promised me you would never tell a soul what I shared with you, but you turned around and did just that, remember, Ms. Woolfolk?"

Carmelita hesitated in responding as blood continued to pour from her mouth. When she tried to speak, cardinal red spittle shot from her lips onto Mayven's shirt. Mayven jumped back, pissed off even more.

"Nasty fucker!"

"She done fucked up your nice shirt, May?" Pinky snickered.

Mayven pursed her lips, and her eyes narrowed as she moved back to her previous position.

"It's cool cause before this is over, she gone spill a lot more."

Monica watched in horror as the situation unfolded right in front of her eyes.

"I didn't do anything," she pleaded. "Please, I won't say nothing, just let me go... I didn't do anything."

Major was sick of hearing her whining. Without a second thought, Major used the butt of his gun and struck Monica in the mouth, caving in her front teeth and busting open her lips. She yelped in pain. Monica wanted to reach for her mouth but she couldn't. Her head fell back from the power of Major's blow.

"Shut the fuck up, damn! Yo ass is guilty by fuckin' association," Major leveled.

Another ripple went through the crowd of bystanders as they cheered Major on. But Mayven was just getting warmed up. The penned up anger she felt for Devereux commingled with the ill-begotten feelings she had stored away for Ms. Woolfolk. Carmelita was going to pay the price for it all.

"You betrayed me..." Mayven's exterior again returned to its original cool state. There was no need to scream at Ms. Woolfolk. Mayven's message was clear, and Carmelita's face showed it.

"That night, no sooner did I spill my soul to you, your black ass went and told the first person you saw. You didn't even know I was there, standing right outside this very same office when you opened your fuckin' mouth about me. You told that bitch everything and then y'all motherfucker's had the nerve to laugh at my pain, at my expense..." Mayven's monotone voice displayed no emotion. She resigned herself to that place of detachment while still tapping into the pain that motivated her.

Carmelita wept openly. When she allowed her mind to focus, she recalled the very night Mayven described. The guilt of what she'd routinely done a thousand times before, negating secrecy and violating emotions, was now coming back to haunt her, face to face. She would pay dearly for the sins of her whispers.

"So, now, Ms. Carmelita Woolfolk," Mayven began, positioning herself again immediately in front of her victim, "every time you look at your deceitful face and your lying mouth, you'll remember what you did to me..."

Like lightning, Mayven manipulated her blade, balancing Carmelita's head with her free hand. One determined slice opened the victims' forehead; scraping the bone beneath it. Before the skin could pucker and the blood seep, Mayven let loose another indiscriminate slice; cutting Carmelita from ear to ear; ripping through the flesh that held her lips together. Blood trailed down Carmelita's face, clouding her eyes and staining her tear soaked cheeks. Her mouth hung open, with no ability to close it. Monica shrieked in horror, and a roar lifted in the group of onlookers as they pushed their way further into the office to get a front row seat.

"Damn May! You vicious as fuck!" Pinky howled, applauding her friends' effort.

May allowed Carmelita's head to drop, falling anyway her neck could hold her.

"Y'all have at that bitch," Mayven said dismissively, as she wiped her blade on Carmelita's jeans and shoved it in the sheath. The crowd parted for Mayven as she exited the office. Major grabbed up the kill kit and exited the office as well.

"You think Pinky can handle it?" He asked as they made their way to the back door.

"Yeah, she got some shit to work out."

Before Mayven and Major could leave the building, the twelve residents piled into the office. Voices yelling, 'get that hoe', 'let me at her', and random screams faded as the back door of Prater House closed.

Chapter Six

The courtroom was stunned after Anna Black's display. Prosecutor Norwood was livid, knowing that her entire case could be undermined by the unpredictable defendant now defender. Her co-prosecutor and first chair, Margot Baptiste caught the brunt of the lead prosecutor's railing.

"This is a fucking nightmare," Norwood seethed.

"Keep your voice down," Baptiste gently chastised, looking around to see who could possibly overhear. Margot was very familiar with Norwood, having worked with her in the prosecutor's office for more than four years now. Attorney Baptists knew that Norwood didn't respond well to being corrected, but Margot had to take the chance.

"Don't you dare shush me," Judith spat. "You just make sure we are ready for this fiasco."

With that, Prosecutor Norwood smoothed down her pinstriped skirt and grabbed her briefcase. She knew the cameras would be waiting for her. Judith put on her poker face and made her way through the crowd, still hulled up in the courtroom. As she passed Detective Phillips and Dr. Daniels, Norwood paused briefly.

"You should have warned me this would happen."

Her words were intended for Chloe as Judith stomped off to meet the press.

"Don't pay her any mind," Michael said, turning to face Chloe. "There's no way you could have known that."

Chloe waved a dismissive hand and prepared to leave the courtroom.

"She's a bit spiteful, don't you agree," Nigel added, standing to his feet after Chloe stood up.

"You can say that again," Chloe sighed.

Michael stood in front of the threesome and made his way to the aisle. He stood in place until Chloe arrived, and proceeded to move her through the crowd. Nigel fell in where he could, attempting to keep up with the twosome. As Phillips and Dr. Daniels crested the top stairs, all cameras moved in their direction, abandoning Prosecutor Norwood mid-sentence.

There was a clamoring, with multiple reporters trying to get their individual and collective attention.

"Detective Phillips!" "Dr. Daniels!"

"What do you make of today's proceedings?"

"Did you see that coming from Anna Black?"

"What about the baby doll killer?"

The questions bled one into the other, making it difficult to determine where one question started and the other stopped.

Neither Dr. Daniels nor Detective Phillips intended to comment on any of them. Nigel found the duo and posted up right next to them, involving himself in the media may lay. As reporters began to recognize who he was, they fielded questions in his direction.

"Dr. Kemp, how are you involved in the case?"

"Are you the new consultant?"

"What do you make of what happened in the courtroom today?"

Always a fiend for attention, Nigel was more than willing to take questions.

"One at a time, please. I will try and answer all your questions, but please, one at a time."

Phillips and Daniels took the opportunity to exit before anyone else raised another question to them. Once clear of the crowd, Chloe reached into her purse to retrieve her cell phone. The court required all phones to be on silent. Chloe wanted to turn the volume back up on her phone and check to see if there were any missed calls. Seeing Chloe attending to her cell, Michael followed suit.

Chloe scrolled through her text messages and mentally made notes of what she needed to follow-up on. There was a voice mail from Addison that Chloe opted to listen to.

"Dr. Daniels, I know you are currently tied up, but as soon as you get a minute, please call me. There may be a break in the baby doll case."

Chloe's face relayed the urgency of the message. Michael looked up.

"What's going on?"

"I'm not sure just yet, but I have to call Addison. She said something about a break in the baby doll case."

"Well, whatcha waiting on," Michael encouraged. "Call her already!"

Chloe smiled at his enthusiasm and hit the speed dial button for Addison, who picked up on the first ring.

"Addison, good news?"

"I think so, Dr. Daniels."

"I'm here with Michael," Dr. Daniels said. "After the day we had in court, we could both use some good news. I'm going to put you on speaker phone, okay?"

Dr. Daniels clicked the line, and Addison greeted Detective Phillips who replied in kind.

"Don't keep us waiting, Addison, what's going on," Michael asked.

"Well, it looks like some homeless man turned in a black patent leather shoe to officers at the last baby doll crime scene."

Michael and Chloe looked hopefully at each other.

"Did they maintain chain of evidence?" "Did they get the witnesses' contact information?" "Were they able to lift any prints?"

Chloe and Michael bombarded Addison with questions.

"Hold on," she interrupted as politely as possible.

"Sorry Addy, we are a little excited," Dr. Daniels offered.

"I understand," Addison replied. "To question 1: Yes, they maintained the chain of evidence. 2: They do have contact information for the witness, and you're going to love it. 3: No word on prints yet, but the shoe was rushed to the lab, and the request was made to expedite."

Dr. Daniels loved how well Addison handled herself. But there was something she wanted to follow up on.

"Addison, question number two. You said we're going to love it?"

"Yes," Addison replied with a smile.

"And why is that," Michael chimed in, equally as curious for a response.

Addison did her best to hide the laugh brimming on her lips; not because of the witnesses' circumstances but because the interview location was so out of the ordinary.

"He wants you all to come to his house to talk with him."

"No problem," Phillips replied.

"Am I missing something," Dr. Daniels inquired.

"No, you're not."

"Then..." Dr. Daniels encouraged.

"He lives under the overpass."

Logan took his time toweling off from his shower as he admired himself in the floor to ceiling mirror in the master bath. Logan flexed his arms, appreciating the cut of his triceps and the firm line of his biceps. His shoulders were rounding out nicely, creating a dramatic contrast with his slim waist. As Logan continued to wipe beads of water from his body, he moved closer to the mirror examining his abdomens. He had a six pack, as they say, but Logan wasn't satisfied. He wanted his muscles to have muscles. Logan would have to increase his abdominal workouts to get the ripped look he desperately desired.

Logan caught himself looking at himself and stopped. His eyes focused in. Even though Logan was pleased with his progress thus far, there was no smile on his face. He wasn't patting himself on the back. His eyes still reflected past hurts and pains. No matter how he sculpted his body, what he actually saw in the mirror was his former self; his former fat, disgusting self. Logan's old wounds continued to haunt him like ghosts in his memory. Logan was locked in his own gaze, as flashes of shaming memories reared their ugly heads; the rejections, the taunting, the laughter... it rang in his ears like a high pitched alarm, cyclical, without end; different voices, different ages under different circumstances, but the laughter at his expense was all the same.

Logan had to physically close his eyes and shake his head to break free from the torturous grip his subconscious held and insist his conscious mind take over. As he opened his eyes, Logan saw himself in the present. He finished drying off and moved into the master bedroom. Logan had a full schedule of appointments at the gym, back to back. He couldn't be late. Logan prided himself on being the best personal trainer

LA Fitness had to offer. Being the best meant always being prompt and prepared.

Logan was relieved to be reporting to the fitness center today instead of to a personal client. As Logan dressed for work, he thought about his last exchange with Suzette, Suzette Burchett. She called him the other night after she did what she promised to do. Suzette was jealous hearted. Logan used that to his greatest advantage. Suzette believed she and Logan had a special connection. She considered Leslie Viega a threat; and so just like any woman scorned, Suzette determined to settle her own personal score. When she called Logan, Suzette sounded surprisingly excited.

"I did it! I told you I would. I took care of her; now we can be together, right?"

At first, Logan wasn't sure what Suzette was talking about, and he asked her to explain herself.

"Explain? Logan, I told you what I was going to do, and I did it. I did it for you baby, for us."

"Tell me, Suzette, I need to hear it from your lips."

"If I tell you, do you promise we can be together?"

Logan fell silent. She didn't like it when he was unresponsive.

"I watched you two as you worked out together that last time. I saw how Leslie looked at you, all doe-eyed. Every chance she got, Logan, she put her hands on you, touching you, feeling on you. I didn't like that, not at all. I waited until you left. I didn't want this to come back on you in any way. Leslie was still in her gym; if you can call a converted garage a real gym. The garage door was still up. Leslie was still showing off in front of the mirrors, so I walked in. You should have seen her face when she saw me. Logan, it was priceless. But I made nice, told her I was in the neighborhood and saw her, and you know started up a little conversation. You know Leslie, she loves to talk about herself, and so I let her."

"What happened next," Logan asked. He was getting a mental and physical rise from the conversation.

"I made some excuse about it being cold in the garage so there would be a reason to close the door. When Leslie's back was turned to me, I grabbed the first thing I saw."

"What was that," Logan asked. It was the details that got him off. He wanted to hear every bit of it.

"It was the jump rope you two used. I saw Leslie flouncing herself all in front of you; barely there top, her humongous breasts bouncing up and down trying to entice you. But I know you weren't impressed. You don't want her.

"What did you do?" Logan's voice was low and seductive, titillating Suzette's already willing ears. She was eager to please him.

"I took the jump rope, and I wrapped it around her puny little neck, and I squeezed. I squeezed so hard."

"What happened next?" Logan's manhood was swollen. He had to touch himself just to find relief.

Suzette giggled a little before she continued.

"Leslie started gagging and kicking and fighting, but I kept the pressure on, squeezing until she stopped."

Logan's stroke intensified. He closed his eyes and laid back on the bed, massaging his engorged member.

"You killed her, over me?" Logan asked.

"Of course I did," Suzette replied quickly. "Leslie refused to see what you and I have together, Logan. She wanted you all to herself. She wouldn't stop until she had you, and I wasn't going to let her. The answer to your question is, yes, I did it for you. So are we still on for next week?"

Logan made a lackluster promise to get her off the phone. He didn't want Suzette to hear him jacking off. Suzette, like Leslie, was the typical gym rat. Blonde and beautiful, starving herself to be thinner. Suzette was one of the women, that had she known him before, would have rejected Logan outright. She wouldn't have given the fat, out of shape Logan a second glance. But now, she killed for him. That sent Logan over the edge, and he exploded; releasing waves of hot gism; reveling in his passive victory.

Logan had what some would call a magic touch. It was a skill he developed when he was in his dark place. Suzette wasn't crazy; she was programmed neurolinguistically. Logan smiled. He regained the power and control those who mistreated him, had on him; the power they had to make him hate himself. Every time one of blonde bombshell gym rats died, he became stronger and stronger; more confident in who he was. They would all pay for what they did to him.

"Another one down... so many more pretty women to go..."

Chapter Seven

Detective Phillips and Dr. Daniels made the decision to try and meet with the witness who delivered the shoe to the officer at the dump site. The courthouse was not far from the interstate, and so the two jumped in Michael's SUV to try and locate him. Addison provided as much of a location as possible; however, neither Phillips nor Daniels could forget the overpass where they found the girl with one shoe. That's where they headed.

"Do you think he'll be there," Dr. Daniels queried.

"Man I hope so," Phillips answered. "We need all the help we can get on this case."

"How will we know who is," Chloe considered.

"I don't know," Michael replied. "He may have to find us."

Although the duo could pretty much pinpoint the right overpass, because of the high rate of homelessness in the metro area, singling out which homeless man was the witness could prove difficult. But Michael and Chloe were prepared to talk to everyone until they found their witness. It didn't take long before Detective Phillips was turning on the blue lights on the truck and pulling the SUV over to the side of the road. Michael made sure to pull up in such a way that his door opened to traffic. After checking his rearview mirror, Detective Phillips exited the truck, closed the door, and walked around the back to the passenger side. He assisted Chloe in getting out of the truck and closed the door behind her.

Regardless of the time of day, being under thick, elevated concrete changed the temperature by a few degrees and practically reduced all available light. It was much like being in a tunnel where on each end you could see the light absent from the actual space you occupied.

Immediately upon exiting the vehicle, Michael and Chloe started looking around for any sign of life. Because of safety issues, those who resided in and around the overpass typically slept in the space created between the overhead street and the slanted concrete slab that extended to the ground. Resultantly, it was necessary for Chloe and Michael to look to the rafters to try and locate their witness.

"Hold on a second," Michael advised, temporarily abandoning Chloe and returning to the truck. Chloe kept her eyes peeled for any movement up top. She barely heard Michael's footsteps moving away from her over the hum and occasional blaring horn of the cars whisking by. When Michael returned, Chloe barely heard it. Instead, she felt a presence behind her and turned to find him there. Her face was pensive, up until that moment and then instantly relieved. Michael handed her a flashlight and kept one for himself.

"Divide and conquer," Chloe suggested.

"No, you stay with me," Michael corrected.

Being in and around the interstate was a dangerous proposition. Detective Phillips had been to far too many accident scenes where a person was injured or killed on the side of the road. He wouldn't risk Chloe being hurt. Chloe switched on her light and Michael did the same. They worked from the middle to one end and then the other in an effort to locate the witness. Having the light available made all the difference. Things they had been unable to detect with the naked eye were revealed when under the focused, incandescent light. Chloe didn't like having to shine the light into the faces of the disenfranchised. It seemed disrespectful and intrusive. Her heart nearly stopped when her light landed on the face of a small child. His skin was dark, but the stains on his face were darker. The child shielded his face when the abrasive light struck his wide eyes; the tattered edges of his jacket sleeve making jagged shadows in the light. Chloe lowered the flashlight not wanting to further offend. But she wanted to see him, reassure the child somehow that everything would be okay. Chloe wanted to make sure he wasn't up there by himself, with no mom or dad to take care of him. Instinctively, she reached for Michael. His gaze followed her light as it traveled upwards and found the child cowering. Michael saw the anguish on Chloe's face.

"I know…"

Although it was painful to see a child in this situation, they knew they had to move on. Chloe promised she wouldn't forget.

He watched them searching from his perch on the opposite side of the highway. It was the pretty lady and her cop friend. Stanley knew they were there for him. But he waited. Maybe they would come to where he was. Maybe Stanley would venture out to meet them. The voices in his head uttered mixed messages, clouding his thoughts, making his head ache. Today was one of those days for Stanley. For now, at least, Stanley was still in touch with who he was. But he wasn't quite ready to reveal himself, not just yet.

Grace's day had been trying enough, but that didn't mean she was absolved of her maternal duties. The children's homework was completed, and dinner was on the table. Much like when she was a child, Grace continued the tradition of the family sitting down to dinner every night regardless. Dinner was nothing fancy; roast beef, mashed potatoes, and sweet peas, but it was a balanced meal, nonetheless. The family was unusually quiet; each lost in their own thoughts. Preston hated sweet peas and pushed them around on his plate, hiding them under the mashed potatoes he still had yet to touch. Drake could barely stand to look down at the other end of the table where his wife sat. He focused on the newspaper he brought to the table; ignoring everyone else. It was Mary Lou who finally initiated conversation.

"Mommy, where's Ms. Madeline?"

Grace nearly choked on the roast beef in her mouth behind her daughter's question. Drake looked up warily.

"Yeah, mom, where is she," Preston chimed in abandoning the green peas sprawled on his plate. "I miss her."

"I do, too," Mary Lou echoed. She looked to her mother for an answer.

Grace politely sat her fork down and cleared her throat. Drake waited for her response as eagerly as the children did.

"She's no longer with us," Grace replied. "Now, let's finish up dinner, shall we?"

"But where is she? Why is she not here," Mary Lou pressed.

Grace felt her cheeks flush, not from embarrassment, but anger. Taking a sip of her water, Grace again tried to refocus the children's inquisition.

"I don't know where she is, Mary Lou. I mean, who could know? She's not working here anymore so please, let's drop the subject and finish dinner."

Mary Lou never liked to be corrected by her mother, and her head fell as her mother spoke.

"But I still miss her…"

"Me, too," Preston added.

Grace slammed the fragile glass down onto the hard wooden table. The base of the glass chipped from the connection.

"That's enough! She's gone! Do you hear me? The help is gone! I don't know where she is. I don't give a damn where she is! She's not here! Do you understand? That nigger is not here!"

"Grace," Drake scolded.

Grace glared in his direction, daring Drake to say anything else. He recognized she was a lost cause and focused his attention on the children.

"Preston, Mary Lou, please excuse yourselves from the table, okay? Mommy and daddy need to have adult talk."

The children did as their father said with no back talk. As the two exited the dining room and made their way toward the back stairs, Grace lit into her insolent husband.

"How dare you correct me in front of them? Don't you dare do that again!"

"Lower your voice," Drake instructed.

"Don't you dare, you bastard," Grace sniped. "Don't!"

Before Drake could speak another word, Grace launched into a full tirade. "And how dare the two of them! Ungrateful little..."

"Don't disparage my children, Grace," Drake demanded.

"They are my kids, too! Ingrates... I'm right here, every day, taking care of them and they question me about the help? They miss those jigaboos; looking all sad and despondent as if somehow those niggers mattered."

Grace cackled.

"The apple didn't fall far from that tree did it, Drake?"

"Excuse me?" Drake interjected.

"Oh, as if you don't know what I mean," Grace decried. "You're a nigger lover, too!"

Drake didn't dignify his wife's verbal assault with a response. He knew Grace would laud his betrayal over his head forever, so there was no point in offering a defense. When he rolled his eyes, Grace picked up the water glass and threw it in Drake's direction. Drake's eyes caught the tail end of something whizzing by, and his ears heard the glass shattering against the wall behind his head.

"Really?"

"Next time I won't miss!" Grace grabbed the knife from the table and held it tightly, tapping the butt end against the wooden surface.

Drake looked curiously in Grace's direction. His head tilted slightly to the left as if somehow seeing her from a different angle would offer greater insight. Drake's desire to go to the other end of the table and choke her bony neck was temporarily sedated as he opted for a much calmer exterior response.

"And if I do, you know, correct you again," Drake began; his voice calm and regulated. "What are going to do, Grace, kill me, too?"

Grace automatically looked over her shoulder to see if her children were still in earshot. When her eyes found her husband again, her eyes were surprisingly soft, yet her words remained laced with venom.

"Don't tempt me..."

Drake refused to be intimidated. He stayed as cold as their sex life.

"See Grace," Drake started, cradling his fingers on the table, "I'm not frail and unsuspecting like the poor girls you murdered."

"Is that some kind of threat, Drake?"

"No, dear," he answered smiling indiscriminately. "I'm not the least bit concerned about you coming after me, trying to kill me in my sleep, or anything of the sort."

Grace threw her hand in his direction, scoffing at his cavalier response. But Drake wasn't finished.

"Remember Grace, I know you. I know that you prey on the weak and vulnerable. I know you pick your battles. I believe you will pick wisely when it comes to me." The knife tapping ceased, but Grace continued to tightly clutch the utensil.

Drake minded his manners and wiped the corners of his mouth with the napkin previously laid across his lap. Calmly, Drake scooted his chair back from the table and stood up. He meandered toward Grace at the opposite end. She didn't bother to look up at him.

When Drake reached her, he briefly paused and leaned down to ensure she didn't miss what he had to say.

"And if you ever talk to or about my children like that again, you will be the one sleeping with one eye open."

It was only then Grace looked up, catching the back of her husband as he quietly exited the dining room. He was brazen, emboldened, and Grace didn't like it. Apparently, Drake had forgotten his place. She would find a way to remind him.

Chapter Eight

Major and Mayven didn't have an accomplice in Major's old house. But that didn't deter the two from concocting a plan to recreate in Brigadoon what happened in Prater House. Brigadoon would be a little more dangerous because men staffed the house. Major peeped the staff earlier when they joined the crowd heading toward the residences. One, he was familiar with, an older gentleman, an asthmatic. He wouldn't be a problem for the duo to overpower but the other guy was much younger, seemed a bit more on top of his game. Major didn't know him. He must have come after Major and Mayven ran away. But Major wasn't fearful. He would take on the younger guy, and once the residents saw what was up, Major was convinced they'd be willing to join in the fun.

Once in position, Mayven made her way to the front door. She broadened her smile and unleashed her long, black mane before knocking. It only took a few seconds before there was a response.

It was the younger man who answered.

"May I help you," he asked; unable to keep his attention on Mayven's face. She helped him by altering her stance, so her ass jutted out a little further.

"Yeah, "Mayven teased. "I need to see Duke."

His eyes were slow to travel to her face. When he found her mouth, his gaze remained on her pouty lips.

"Duke?"

"Yeah, I need to see him. Can I come in?"

Mayven took a slight step forward, rolling her hips before positioning herself within striking distance.

"Sorry, babe," He began, not retreating from her advances, "I can't let girls in here." He smiled and leaned against the door jam, fully engaged in the flirt.

"But he asked me to come by," Mayven whined. "Please, can I come in for just a minute? I promise this won't take long."

She smiled. He smiled and chuckled. He was flattered. She was fine. Mayven stepped even closer, completely eradicating the distance between her and the staff person. His smile widened. Major held his position on the side of the building; keeping both parties within his sights. He was ready to move. Mayven slid her hand to her sheath while the man in the doorway ogled her. He never heard the snap that released her blade and was barely able to respond before Mayven had the steel to his neck. That's when Major made his move, meeting his girl in the entryway to Brigadoon. His gun was already raised, and Major pushed the muzzle to the man's forehead.

"You was eyeballin' my girl, huh, nigga?"

The staffer's eyes were as big as his smile once was.

"Naw, man, naw," he quickly denied.

"I seen you motherfucka' now back it up. We comin' in."

The staffer had little choice but to back up as instructed. Mayven didn't relinquish the pressure on the blade until Major was in play. It didn't take long before some of the residents of Brigadoon took note of what was happening.

"Hell naw! They got Jenkins ass," one kid yelled from the hallway as Jenkins was backed into the common area. The layout of all the houses was exactly the same. Been in one, you've been in them all. Malcolm Jenkins was pushed back into the staff office. With the kill kit on deck, Major and Mayven made quick work of locking him down to the chair. Jenkins looked too shocked to verbally protest. The cut to his neck from Mayven's pressured blade convinced him protestation might not be the best idea. The yelling from one resident turned into full rebel-rousing from each one who learned of Jenkins fate. It was the increased noise level that made Mr. Cornelius Franklin speed up in the bathroom.

"Can't step away for a minute without somebody going off," Cornelius said aloud, quickly running his soapy hands under the lukewarm water and grabbing for the last paper towel on the roll. Ordinarily, he would replace the towels and spend a lot more time thoroughly washing his hands, but the ruckus outside didn't allow for such luxuries. Double checking to make sure his inhaler was still in his pants pocket, Mr. Franklin hurriedly exited the bathroom and made his way down the hall towards the communal area.

"Slow down, young man," Mr. Franklin called out after a resident who side-swiped him in the corridor. The young man never looked back as his focus was on the drama unfolding in the front of the house. Mr. Franklin's attention was focused there as well. When he finally crested the top of the hallway, Mr. Franklin's mouth fell open. Nearly every resident was in the common area, standing on chairs, and the dining room table. They were screaming and yelling any number of obscenities. Mr. Franklin felt his chest start to tighten.

"If you don't get down from there," he instructed the first young man he came to. Mr. Franklin reached for the young man, grabbing him by the back of the shirt. When the young man felt someone tugging on him and then turned and saw it was a staff person, the resident let his elbow fly back, connecting with the bridge of Mr. Franklin's nose. Wincing in pain, Cornelius' hands immediately flew to the pain as blood began to seep from the break. His eyes watered from the sting. Mr. Franklin's chest tightened more as his available air supply decreased.

"Jenkins, you scared?"

Major felt like fuckin' with the young cat. Even though Mayven was set out to tease him, Major didn't like the way Jenkins responded.

"Whatchu think," Malcolm replied. He may have been duct taped to a chair, but he wasn't no punk.

"I think you motherfuckin bleedin', bitch."

Mayven didn't like Jenkins disposition. He was still acting cocky, fronting like he wasn't afraid. Mayven let her blade fly and with every connection, sliced Jenkins wide open. She didn't care where her steel landed, as long as she made contact and as long as he felt pain. As blood began to surface, Mayven sliced one more time for the hell of it.

Malcolm did his best to hold it together, but the assault to his body was relentless. A scream brimmed on his quivering lips. The sting of tears pressing to fall nearly matched the sting from Mayven's blade. Major leaned in close, watching the transformation of Jenkins' face. He liked to see the pain, not just inflict it. Major found the physical metamorphosis fascinating.

"How you feelin' now, playa," Major asked teasingly.

Jenkins desperately fought the urge to cry out, as the depths of his injuries began to manifest.

The noise level from outside the office increased and caught Mayven's attention. The residents hooped and hollered as they saw a stumbling and bleeding Mr. Franklin making his way to the office. All the residents except one. Maurice Brown didn't like what was going on. He didn't think it was right. Cowering in the corner, Maurice tried to find a way out. Mr. Jenkins and Mr. Franklin needed some help. He was afraid that before long, he and the other residents would, too.

"He fucked up now, ain't he," one of the other boy's called out.

"Hell yeah, man," another replied.

Mr. Franklin didn't respond to the taunts. His goal was to get to the office and get to the phone. He had no idea what was waiting for him.

Logan was one of the more popular fitness trainers at the gym. There was always a waiting list with new clients eager to sign up for any available work out slot Logan had. His private sessions were, of course, the most popular. Logan had an unexpected opening and smiled as he posted it to the information bulletin board. Scantily clad women flocked to the board to see.

"Logan! Logan," was all he heard as he moved through the group after posting. There were some clients and potential customers who were more aggressive than others and followed him as he made his way to the staff locker room.

"Logan, what do I have to do to get personal service," Charlie, one of his longstanding center clients asked. When she pulled him by the shoulder from behind, Logan stopped long enough to address her. Charlie Simpkins was an older client; much older than Logan was used to dealing with. But she reminded him of all the buxom bimbo-blondes who so readily dismissed him before he became the Logan they currently saw.

Charlie was standing way too close; obliterating Logan's personal space. Her perfume was too strong and her inflated breasts pressed against his chest. Logan longed to step back and gain some breathing room, but Charlie never released her grip on his shoulder.

Logan smiled defensively, unsure how to respond.

"Come on sweetie, you've made me wait a long time."

Charlie's eyes were smoldering in an old woman trying to be young kind of way.

Beth Ann watched the old lady pushing herself on Logan. *...so disrespectful...* Beth Ann thought as she moseyed over closer to the duo. She didn't intend to interrupt, but she wanted to be close enough to hear what was being said. Beth Ann had been with Logan just about as long as Charlie, and she too desired to have private time with him. If Logan gave Charlie a heads up, Beth Ann wanted it as well.

"Just fill out the questionnaire, Charlie, that's all you have to do," Logan advised, still trying to gain distance between them.

"And there's nothing I can do to get ahead of the crowd?"

Charlie was brazen enough to take her free hand and trace Logan's chest with it. He visibly pulled away and Beth Ann physically advanced; her eyes slit as the envious green-eyed monster reared its jealous head.

"No, Ms. Charlie, there's nothing you can do. Now if you would excuse me?"

Logan found a way to break away from the overzealous client. She called after him, but Logan sped up to get to safety in the locker room. Beth Ann made a point of giving Charlie the evil eye to her face as she walked by her.

"What's your problem," Charlie mumbled under her breath as the two crossed paths. Beth Ann didn't verbally respond, but she wouldn't forget how Charlie threw herself at Logan.

No one stood out as the potential witness. No one came forward and said, 'hey, I'm the one who found the shoe. I'm the one you need to talk to'. There were plenty of societal nobodies under the overpass, but Dr. Daniels and Detective Phillips had so far been unsuccessful in rooting out who they came to see.

"Let's check the other side," Michael suggested, as the two made their way back to the SUV. Chloe paused again as they neared the place where she saw the small child.

"There's nothing you can do about it right now," Michael offered.

She knew what Michael said was true, but that didn't make Chloe feel any better. When Michael opened the door, Chloe entered the truck and sat down. She had such mixed feelings; hopeful about finding the witness and maybe making headway on the case, but completely disheartened by the raw truth of those who lived under the overpass. Michael rounded the truck, got in placing the flashlights behind the seat, and started the vehicle. Naturally, he looked in Chloe's direction. Her wayward glance found him and their eyes connected. There was concern and sadness in Chloe's eyes that pricked Michael's heart. He could see the effect this situation had on her. Quite out of character, Michael extended his hand to her. It was a risk. Chloe could reject him outright, but Michael took the chance.

Chloe saw his extended hand. She knew it was more than a supportive gesture. There was so much about it that felt right, though, and she gently slid her hand into his. When Michael covered her hand with his own, there was a settling in Chloe's spirit; a familiarity that comforted her. Michael's heart skipped a decisive beat as he felt the warmth of her touch in a way he never experienced before. Michael knew she had a brilliant mind. He knew Chloe had a good heart. This was the first time he felt it beat in sync with his. A smile creased his lips as he put on the blinker to pull the SUV back into traffic.

It didn't take long before Detective Phillips found a place to exit the interstate and re-enter on the other side. Traffic was better in the eastbound direction, and as such, the two were parked under the overpass in just a few minutes. It was only then their hands separated. A warm smile between them was exchanged as Detective Phillips exited the car. Opening the rear door, Michael grabbed the flashlights before making his way to help Chloe out of the vehicle.

Once Detective Phillips and Dr. Daniels were successfully out of the SUV, with flashlights turned on, the two began to walk the underpass in search of the witness. Chloe moved with trepidation, hesitant to see another child much like the last. She didn't want to see another child in the same condition. Not that it was easier to see adults who had nothing or seemingly had nothing, it was just very, very hard for Chloe to see a child in such a predicament. Instead of moving separately, the duo moved together. There were not as many people residing at the top of the overpass on this side of the highway. In some ways that was relieving; in other ways, it was not. The fewer people available, however, the less likely Detective Phillips and Dr. Daniels were in finding their witness.

Stanley wanted to do the right thing. He liked the lady, and the guy she was with didn't seem too bad. He could tell the officer cared about the doctor lady. For Stanley, that was important. The officer's expressed kindness to the lady would make Stanley much more comfortable in talking in front of the both of them. But the voices in his head were sending mixed signals, confusing what it is that he wanted to say; whether Stanley wanted to say anything at all. Maybe he had done enough by giving them the shoe? They were smart people. They should be able to put two and two together to find the woman that threw that poor girl out like trash.

Stanley knew that coming forward would mean his life would not be the same. He would literally be coming out of the shadows. The ghosts from his past would be revisited, and not just by him at night when he couldn't sleep. Stanley's old life would be on display. His fellow co-workers, students the university community would see just how far he had fallen. Maybe if he told them what they needed to hear, it would just be this one conversation, and he could go back to his life, his comfortable life living under the overpass. To revisit his history would mean revisiting pains Stanley had long since tried to drown out. But what if they wanted more from him? What if they wanted Stanley to testify; be out in front of the cameras, and have people actually see him?

To look at Stanley, you wouldn't know it, but he had a family. Stanley had a wife and children; at least he used to. His mother and father were still alive, at least the last time he was in touch with anybody. How long had it been since he saw his family? It was easy to lose track of time when you lived on the street. Days ran into each other, nights overlapped. But Stanley was pretty good about watching the moon and stars and keeping track of time in that way. The year? That was a little bit more difficult. When Stanley allowed himself to be around other people or venture into an area where he could overhear a radio or listen to a conversation, Stanley got tidbits of information to let him know what was really going on in the world. It was a big world out there; yet, Stanley made it small enough to manage.

They were close now. Stanley had to make a decision whether to talk to them or not.

As the two made their way under the darkened overpass, not much was panning out. Then, Detective Phillips saw movement ahead of them. Chloe paused when he blocked her forward advancement. It was hard to tell in the shadowy darkness who it was; whether a woman or a man. Although it may have been rude to shine the light in the face of the person coming their way, Michael's detective instinct took over. He lifted the light to see who it was. Maybe it was who they were looking for. When the light finally hit the face of the one approaching, his or her hands went immediately up and covered their eyes. Their steps halted temporarily. Detective Phillips slowly advanced, reaching for his badge with his free hand; ever mindful of his service revolver.

The moment was tense. Chloe felt her heart rate increase. Detective Philips resisted the urge to yell, 'Stop! Police!' If this was the witness, yelling that way would most likely frighten him off. At the same time, the situation was precarious at best.

"Get that light outa my face!"

Detective Philips and Dr. Daniels relaxed a bit after hearing the high pitched voice. This was not their witness. As the woman continued to move towards them, Michael offered an apology. The lady, layered in tattered clothing and slightly bent over, probably from carrying the weight of the world on her shoulders, blew the detective off. She mumbled something they couldn't understand and proceeded on her way. Chloe breathed a sigh of relief, but the encounter reminded her of how dangerous this kind of work could be. Michael checked in with her to make sure she was okay, and the two decided to continue their search.

He had been lurking and watched the confrontation with Bea; a lady that lived not too far from him. Pushing pass the conflicting voices in his head, Stanley decided to reveal himself. He saw that the officer could be quick on the draw, so Stan was careful as he began his descent from the upper echelon of the underpass. This time it was Chloe who saw suspicious movement. She caught up the few steps to Michael who was slightly ahead of her, and once she got his attention, pointed in the direction of the person slowly sliding down the concrete slope. Chloe lifted her light; not to the individual's face, but to the slope, illuminating it. Michael's hand naturally fell to the butt of his gun but he demonstrated restraint in advancing or announcing.

When the man finally landed on the asphalt, he put his hands up, signifying that he came in peace. Dr. Daniels and Detective Phillips held their position. The light in Chloe's hand continued to brighten his path as he drew closer. The traffic noise behind them died down. When Stanley felt he was close enough to be heard, he spoke.

"I-I-I think you're looking for me..."

Chapter Nine

He was still in a significant amount of pain, but as he neared the office, Mr. Franklin's eyes grew exponentially wider.

"Wh-wh-what are you doing in here?"

His breathing was labored, and he fumbled to find the inhaler he had tucked away. When Major heard the familiar voice, he stopped playing with Jenkins and turned to face Mr. Franklin.

"Cornelius, my old friend," Major said smilingly.

The sentiment was not mutual. When Mr. Franklin looked up into the face of one of his former residents, he was frightened. When he saw the gun Major wielded, Cornelius was petrified. He remembered Major, and not in a good way. Mr. Franklin finally found his inhaler. Shakily removing the cap, he put the breathing apparatus to his mouth. As he took in a deep breath and compressed the button to activate the medicine. To Mr. Franklin's surprise, the inhaler was abruptly slapped from his hand.

"You won't be needing that," Major advised, knocking the inhaler to the ground. He walked over to Mr. Franklin, laced his arm around Cornelius' neck and escorted him the rest of the way into the office. Jenkins eyed the walkie-talkie, sitting in the holder on the office desk. He knew he couldn't get to it to call for help. It was like a beacon, off in the distance, he couldn't quite reach. And now it looked like his partner wouldn't be able to get to it either. The residents continued to raise hell in the backdrop. Mayven sat on the desk and watched as Major ushered his old nemesis to the available office chair. Major didn't need any help in lassoing the much frailer Mr. Franklin. Unlike Mr. Jenkins, Cornelius didn't hesitate to beg for his life.

"Now, Major... I'm not sure what this is about... but please, whatever you're thinking... don't do this... please..."

Major continued to wrap the last of the duct tape around Mr. Franklin. Mayven watched as the muscles in Major's jawline flexed repeatedly. She knew what it meant.

There were times when Major wasn't long on conversation. This was one of those times. As Mr. Franklin continued to whimper and try to reason with his assailant, Major quietly fumed. Major thought about their joined past and how he resented Mr. Franklin; the man who was always talking about his perfect family, his perfect sons – he had two, right around the age of the boys he worked with...throwing his boys success up in the face of the residents as something they should aspire to. Mr. Franklin looked down on the residents and always tried to make an example out of them and their deleterious behavior. They would never be as good as his faultless sons; the boys Mr. Cornelius relentlessly lauded over the resident's heads. He was sanctimonious and entitled and Major hated him for it.

Raw rage boiled up from Major's underbelly and exploded on Mr. Franklin. The butt of Major's pistol was his weapon of choice as he brutally beat Cornelius about the head and face. You could hear the cracking of Mr. Franklin's skull and then the dull thud when the bones caved in. Blood squirted and then leaked as Cornelius gasped for air. His wheezing made for an eerie echo to the brute force with which Major swung his gun. Animalistic grunts poured from Major's lips as he remembered all the times he was made to feel small by the man he was currently beating into submission.

Mayven giggled at the sight and the residents who were privy to the assault squealed with excitement; marking each sadistic blow with cat calls and adulations of approval. Except one...

While everyone's attention was on what was happening in the office, Maurice lifted himself from the corner he cowered in. He did his best to be inconspicuous as he tiptoed behind the dining room table. When he felt he was in the clear, Maurice bolted for the front door. He had to get help and he had to get it now. One of the other residents saw Maurice leaving the scene and alerted.

"Maurice ran! Oooo! Maurice ran!"

Mayven leaped from the desk but not before Major abandoned Mr. Franklin and bolted for the door. This kid could ruin everything. By the time Mayven made it out of the office, Major was already outside pursuing the young man.

"HELP! GOD, PLEASE! SOMEBODY HELP!"

Maurice was screaming at the top of his lungs. His begging echoed across campus gaining ground as it went.

"Shut the fuck up!" Major called from behind, but Maurice was too afraid to listen.

"HELP! HELP! PLEASE, HELP US!"

Maurice turned and saw Major coming at him fast. His feet slipped on the grassy surface but Maurice didn't quit. He kept running. He kept screaming for help. His voice was starting to gain traction as lights turned on. Major was in hot pursuit, gaining ground on the spry teen.

"MAJOR!"

It was Mayven. He needed to know people were paying attention. Major stopped running.

"HELP! PLEASE, HE—

Maurice's voice was permanently silenced as the steel bullet pierced the back of his cranium and exited his right eye. The echo of the shot ricocheted through campus... no longer Maurice's voice.

Tanner Sr. made the difficult decision to contact the police department and file a missing person's report on his daughter, Tangela. He didn't know what else to do. At the hotel, the night before, he watched his son, Tanner Jr., toss and turn late into the midnight hour. Junior was worried. He was worried about his sister. Tanner Sr. provided as much information to the operator as possible. When she asked how long Tangela had been missing, Tanner realized he really didn't know. The operator sounded less than enthusiastic or concerned about the missing person's report. Maybe it was the nature of the job; maybe she was just tired, Tanner didn't know. Before the call was discontinued, the operator asked if there was anything else he thought would aid them in the case.

"Tangela's car is missing, too," he began. "It was not at her apartment. We can't find it anywhere."

Tanner Sr. provided the make and model of the car. He knew the information he gave the operator was on an ordinary vehicle, so it probably wouldn't be very helpful.

"Do you, by chance, know the license plate number, sir," the operator inquired.

"Hold on one second."

Tanner Sr. scrambled for his wallet. He wasn't sure if the information was still in there but he checked just the same. There were more folded papers in his wallet than Tanner remembered, but he rummaged through them while pacifying the operator that it would only be a second. He was looking for a receipt. Tangela was having a hard time financially and needed help with paying for her state license tags. This was one of the only times she readily asked for assistance. Tanner Sr. was more than happy to help his daughter. He thought he kept the receipt in his wallet.

"Come on; I know it's in here..."

Tanner unfolded several pieces of paper trying to find it. He was a packrat of sorts and knew he needed to do better.

"Got it," he yelled far too loudly in the phone. He apologized to the operator and then read her the number.

"OHD3295..."

The three were finally standing face to face. Stanley still had his hands raised as though surrendering. Detective Phillips encouraged the man to let them down.

"What was your name again," Detective Phillips asked, attempting to make the witness more comfortable.

"... Stanley... Stanley Lucas..."

Cars sped down the interstate causing an elevation in the noise level. Phillips tried to compensate by cupping his hand over his mouth to ask the next question, but he could tell by Mr. Lucas' posture that he was having a hard time hearing him.

"Is there some place we can go to talk," Dr. Daniels asked. She too had to project for Mr. Lucas to hear her. The flashlights were kept at such a level as to not offend Mr. Lucas but to illuminate the conversation nonetheless. Stanley gestured to the two and turned and walked towards the edge of the shelter. The canvas of darkness faded as they walked to the side of the concrete overhang. There was a thin, tall piece of boarding leaning against the wall at an angle. Dr. Daniels could see it was a makeshift cover for a shopping cart she assumed belonged to Mr. Lucas.

"Is this better," Mr. Lucas asked, still finding it necessary to raise his voice. It was some better but not sufficient to conduct an interview. Detective Phillips asked another question that the witness still didn't completely hear. Phillips closed the distance between himself and the witness. Initially, Mr. Lucas took a cautious step back, but Phillips reassured him he meant no harm.

"Would you be willing to ride with us down to the police station?"

Chloe could see the concern rise in the face of Mr. Lucas. He began to adjust his layers of clothing and nervously smooth down his hair. The voices in his head were screaming, no, that he shouldn't go with these people.

"Well," Mr. Lucas began, "I'm not really, you know, presentable to be going around folks."

Detective Phillips understood the witnesses position, but conversing where they stood was insufficient. He looked to Chloe for assistance.

"Well, Mr. Lucas, how would you feel about grabbing a cup of coffee, maybe something to eat, right here in the neighborhood?"

She could see his wheels turning, like maybe her suggestion might be plausible.

"I promise we won't go far," Dr. Daniels reassured.

Again, Stanley took a minute to consider. He didn't like to leave where he was comfortable and he certainly didn't like to leave his belongings. But the growl in his stomach suggested strongly he may need to take these people up on their offer. They seemed decent enough.

Stanley nodded his head, affirming he would go.

"Not far, right," he asked for reassurance.

"Not far, Mr. Lucas, promise," Dr. Daniels reassured.

Detective Phillips led the trio back under the overpass and to his awaiting vehicle. He ensured everyone was securely seated before pulling the truck back out into traffic. He discreetly cracked the windows as the malodorous wave emanating from Mr. Lucas' person filled the truck. As promised, Phillips found a fast food restaurant not far from the interstate and pulled into the parking lot. Michael looked to Chloe. She seemed to have been better at engaging the witness.

"Is this okay, Mr. Lucas," Dr. Daniels inquired.

Mr. Lucas looked up inspecting the restaurant. "I s'pose."

"Would you be comfortable going inside?"

Stanley wasn't too sure about that. Going inside meant encountering more people. There was an audible rumble from his empty belly that could be heard by anyone listening.

"I guess we have our answer," Dr. Daniels smiled, lightening the mood. Detective Phillips took his cue and turned off the ignition. He opened the back passenger door for the witness and went around to assist Dr. Daniels. Although Mr. Lucas lagged slightly behind, the three entered the restaurant.

"Order whatever you like Mr. Lucas," Detective Phillips offered. He didn't have to say it twice. Stanley assessed the menu. The smells inside the restaurant caused the rumbling in his stomach to magnify.

"I'll have two of those, one for now and one for later, some fries, a strawberry milkshake and a large cup of coffee in a to-go cup. Now if you all will excuse me?"

Dr. Daniels watched as Mr. Lucas made his way to the men's restroom. Once the food was purchased, Detective Phillips and Dr. Daniels found a table near the back of the restaurant and waited for Mr. Lucas to return.

Stanley waited until the bathroom was empty, checking the stalls to make sure he was alone. There was a lock on the main door that he slid into place. He could feel his anxiety rising, so he balanced his hands on the porcelain sink. It had been a while since Stanley saw how he looked to the rest of the world. Generally, he avoided mirrors, knowing the reflection he would see would be disconcerting. But he chose to look up, under the fluorescent lights, in the small of the space he now stood in. His beard was scragglier than he recalled and his hair was nappy. There were heavy bags under his eyes like the bags he sometimes carried. It was his eyes, though, that transfixed him. Stanley had seen too much, yet his eyes were surprisingly bright. They failed to show the confusion in his mind or the pain in his heart.

Stanley disconnected from his figure reflected above and turned on the faucet. Gathering a few paper towels and folding them over on themselves, Stanley created a makeshift rag he used to wash his face. He pumped soap into his hands and washed them thoroughly before adding more soap and warm water to again wash his face. A few more towels were used to dry himself, and one last one, Stanley used to unlock the door and turn the handle. He looked around the restaurant and headed in the direction of the two people waiting for him.

The quiet conversation Chloe and Michael were having ended as Mr. Stanley slid into the booth seat. The food on the tray was all for him, and Detective Phillips slid it in the witnesses direction to indicate so. Before beginning, Stanley made the sign of the cross; first touching his forehead, and then closed his eyes and bowed his head. Respectfully, Chloe and Michael followed suit. Stanley prayed silently and when he was done, said amen. Only then did Michael and Chloe lift their heads to see Stanley repeating the Catholicized ritual again.

Dr. Daniels understood Mr. Lucas was a bit skittish about talking to them, and understandably so. But he did seem to respond better to her, so Chloe initiated the conversation in a way she hoped was unassuming.

"Mr. Lucas?"

Stanley looked up from his food in response.

"I don't mean to be insensitive..."

"Don't be concerned with that, young lady," Mr. Lucas began. "If you want to know something, you should ask. If I don't like the question, I won't answer."

Chloe and Michael appreciated his candor and they both offered their own version of an 'understood' smile. Dr. Daniels proceeded; still, she didn't want to offend.

"Mr. Lucas, how long have you been homeless?" Dr. Daniels hated the question even as she raised it.

"Homelessness is a matter of perspective, young lady."

She liked him more and more. Mr. Lucas had a quick wit.

Mr. Lucas didn't bother to look up. Instead, he took a hefty bite of his sandwich. Once he had chewed sufficiently, he expounded on his reply.

"The overpass is my home, at least for now."

"Where did you live before that," Michael asked; trying to reposition himself with Stanley so the witness didn't think Michael wanted to talk to him only for the answers Stanley could provide.

"Not far from where they found that other body."

It took both Chloe and Michael a moment to try and determine where Stanley was referring to. Mr. Lucas saw their struggle and offered an assist.

"That's why I made the decision to take the shoe over there," Mr. Lucas began. "Sometimes, when I can't sleep or just need to reminisce, I go back to my old stomping ground."

It was starting to come together.

"So you went to one of the colleges off Ralph David Abernathy," Detective Phillips asked.

Mr. Lucas looked up and into the eyes of Detective Phillips.

"You surprised, officer?"

Mr. Lucas didn't sound rebuffed by the question; rather checking to see whether Phillips would be rebuffed by his reply. Detective Phillips wasn't quite sure how to respond. A yes to the question would be judgment based on visual evidence. A response of no could sound superficial if he didn't frame it in just the right way. Mr. Lucas smiled intuitively as the voices in his head receded with actual in-person conversation. He was feeling much like his old self. He enjoyed teasing the young man, much to the chagrin of the doctor.

"Not only did I attend, I was a professor," Mr. Lucas replied.

Dr. Daniels and Detective Phillips found it difficult to hide their surprise. His answer begged the obvious question, but before either of them could raise it, Mr. Lucas provided an answer.

"I loved teaching. Seeing young minds grasping concepts previously foreign to them. But it got hard when the voices in my own head overshadowed the words coming from my lips."

Dr. Daniels immediately understood. Not wanting to press in that direction any more than Professor Lucas may have been comfortable with, she shifted the conversation.

"Do you have family, professor?"

He smiled, appreciating the reference. But his smile was short lived when considering the question.

"Not quite sure how to answer that one, young lady," Mr. Lucas offered. "I have a family; a wife and a couple of children... at least I had them before I left."

"How long ago was that," Detective Phillips inquired.

"It's been a few years now...more than I care to remember or can recall some days..."

The trio was silent for a few moments, each partaking in their own thoughts. Detective Phillips waited until Mr. Lucas was well into his meal before interrupting.

"Mr. Lucas, will you tell us how you got the shoe?"

Stanley felt a lot better since his hunger pangs subsided. Taking a sip of the milkshake and then wiping the corners of his mouth, Stanley was prepared for the real reason they were all together.

"I saw her..."

Dr. Daniels perked up and leaned in without encroaching on Mr. Lucas' space. She didn't want to make him uncomfortable, but this confirmation was everything.

"Her?" Phillips gently prodded.

"Yes, her..."

He felt the same kind of exhilaration he knew Chloe did. For the first time since this case began, they at least knew the gender of the baby doll killer.

Phillips didn't want to bombard Mr. Lucas with questions, but he found it difficult to quell his excitement. Chloe noticed it and felt it as they were sitting side by side at the small table. Gently placing a hand on his thigh, Dr. Daniels took over the conversation. Michael could hardly focus; his intentions immediately sidetracked by her feminine touch. He relaxed in his chair as Dr. Daniels continued the conversation.

"Mr. Lucas," Dr. Daniels began, ensuring her voice was soft and only offering as much eye contact as was returned. "Can you walk us through what happened?"

"I can," Mr. Lucas began. He finished up the last of his meal and tucked away the sandwich he was saving for later.

"It was a white woman, thin from what I could see. Couldn't tell how old she was. The lights from traffic made that hard. But from what she was driving, a minivan of some sort, I would guess she has some kids, probably a husband. It was a nice van, not cheap..." Mr. Lucas reached for his cup of coffee and opened the lid, allowing the steam to rise. He blew on it to cool before sipping. His fingerless gloved hands cradled the cup as he continued.

"I want ya'll to catch her. She's not a nice person... that's why I decided when I found the shoe, to turn it over. That wasn't an easy decision for me. I don't deal with people too much... but when I saw how she dumped that poor child... and then drove off with not a care in the world? Nobody deserves that kind of treatment. I saw her, plain... not her face but her. She kicked that bag out of her van. Of course, I didn't know what it was at the time, but, when I went down and saw that shoe that hadn't been there right before, I knew it was nothing good... So I need ya'll to catch that woman... she is not a nice person..."

Chapter Ten

Detective Moore buried herself in her work. The blow-up she had with Lynette weighed heavily on her, but she couldn't allow her personal drama to dominate her thoughts and interfere with the business at hand. The pressure from the chief, the press, the community and anyone else who knew of the triple homicide wore Moore down. She was grateful for the support and cohesiveness of the investigative team, brought about by Tucker being on board. The difference in the level of teamwork was like night and day. Moore was the designated lead on the investigation, but everyone knew it was Buck Tucker who brought the team together.

Everyone was working hard, trying to put the pieces of the puzzle together. It goes without saying, the coroner ruled the murders a homicide. Given the egregious nature in which the victims were killed, more than one killer was suspected. Trying to determine why the victims were chosen was the focus of the investigative team's collective effort. The victims were no angels. They had sordid pasts. With the youngest victim, Mimi Williams being pregnant at the time she was killed, there was speculation as to whether the father of the baby could be determined; and if so, was he in some way involved.

Every drug dealer and pusher in Aiken was under scrutiny. Many had gone further underground when the murders happened. They were links in the chain and didn't want their illicit activities interrupted. It felt like a dead end. Maybe it was. But there was another angle Detective Moore pursued. Shortly after the murders, correspondence was sent to the state's child welfare agency. Thelma Williams had been a foster parent for a long time and guardian to a few children in her care. It may have been a shot in the dark, but at the least, Detective Moore could learn more about the victim as a result of the inquiry. Moore knew, despite the circumstances, the state was historically slow in moving. She made a few phone calls; even the chief got on the phone to try and expedite the process. In the meantime, Moore hoped the efforts of some of her fellow detectives were paying off in greater dividends.

Moore met Tucker at their regular jaunt. Tucker was busy preparing his coffee, but Moore knew, that's where he went to do some deep thinking.

She hoped his thoughts were about the case. Fatima made her coffee and waited. She also knew Tucker wasn't long on frivolous conversation, and whatever the conversation was, it was best initiated by him. Moore busied herself with her cup of Joe and waited for Tucker to speak.

"Wells and Mawley are out rounding up Paco," Tucker said flatly.

"Paco? I thought he would have been gone underground by now," Moore answered.

"Where's he gonna go? We know everybody he's connected to," Tucker smirked. "Besides, Paco is old and slow now."

"Yeah," Moore laughed, "the geriatric dope man."

The two stood side by side, rehashing what they knew so far, which wasn't much. Not long after, Detectives Vicky Wells and Dan Mawley walked in with Paco in tow.

"Put him in interrogation room one," Tucker called out.

"You want to handle this one," Moore asked.

"We can do him together," Tucker confirmed.

Both of the officers freshened their cups before walking down the hall to meet with the witness, suspect; they weren't quite sure how to classify

Paco. That would be determined based on what he had to say.

Mawley and Wells held up their end of the bargain by rooting Paco out. Now it was up to Moore and Tucker to find out what he knew, if anything. Wells and Mawley exited the interrogation room as Tucker and Moore entered. Paco immediately dropped his head on his hands when he saw who was there to talk with him.

"What's the matter, Paco," Moore asked as she pulled up a chair. Tucker preferred to stand in the corner. He found himself to be more intimidating that way. "Don't like the company," Moore asked.

Paco lifted his head slightly and made eye contact with Moore.

"Hell no." Paco immediately put his head back down on his folded hands.

Detective Moore looked back at Tucker, and they exchanged a grin. She returned her attention to the man sitting in front of her.

"Miquel Felipe Oturra," Detective Moore rattled off.

"How the hell you get Paco out of that?" Tucker jeered.

"Not sure, Tuck, maybe Miquel here would like to explain."

Paco rocked his head back and forth on his hands. He had a bad headache, and the officer's conversation was grating his fragile nerves. Paco knew they were trying to goad him into talking.

When Miquel remained unresponsive, the officers pressed harder.

"I dunno, Tucker," Officer Moore began, "maybe if we go pull his file, maybe there's a warrant out for his arrest, an old case we can reopen..."

Everyone in the room knew Miquel didn't want that.

"Bueno, okay," he replied, lifting his head. "What do you want?"

"Fred Connors," Officer Tucker called out.

"Thelma Williams," Moore joined in.

"Mimi Williams," Tucker continued.

"Oh and don't forget her unborn baby," Moore added.

Paco looked from one to the other. The movement made his head pound worse. His eyes grew bigger as they rattled off the names.

"No, no ese," Paco objected. "Is that what you pulled me in here for?"

"Well, yeah, Paco," Tucker advised. He raised himself from the corner and approached the table, leaning over and firmly placing both hands on it.

"So start talking."

"I know nothing ese, nada." Paco was vehement in his denial. That only made the officers more suspicious instead of less. Now it was Moore's turn.

"Paco, we know you didn't do the murders, that's not your style."

"That's right, amiga, I'm nonviolent!"

"But that doesn't make you innocent, Paco," Moore continued.

"So we need to know when was the last time you dealt to them," Tucker confirmed.

Paco grabbed his stomach doubling over.

"I don't feel so good," he mumbled.

"This won't take long, as long as you answer all our questions," Tucker replied.

"Seriously, bro, I don't feel so good," Paco repeated.

"What you got the DT's?" Moore chided.

"Shouldn't be using your own supply," Tucker commented.

Paco heard their comments, but the uproar in his stomach drowned out their noise. He began to dry heave.

"Oh, hell naw," Moore said, getting up from her chair and grabbing the trash can.

"Don't you fuck up this floor!" Tucker yelled.

Paco's dry heaves continued. He grabbed the trash can from the officer just in time. Moore went for the door. Paco didn't stop convulsing until the contents of his belly erupted through his mouth and nose.

"Ah damn!" Tucker said, turning his head in disgust.

Fatima was a sympathetic vomiter and just hearing him heave was enough to turn her stomach upside down. Moore stepped out into the hallway. She probably looked silly to any onlookers who saw her with her hands covering her ears. She hummed to drown out the noise.

Tucker was equally as disgusted as Moore, but his constitution was stronger. He temporarily left the room. When he saw Moore's antics, he burst out laughing. Only then did Fatima uncover her ears.

"Seriously," Tucker jested.

"Hey man, I would have gone right along with him. You don't want that," Moore replied, trying her best to defend without embarrassment.

"You're right, I don't."

Tucker looked around.

"Hey, Landowski," Tucker called; getting the blondes' attention. When she realized who it was, Joan was more than responsive.

"What can I do you for," Joan grinned, pushing out her bosom.

"Can you grab the Lysol and a new trashcan for the interrogation room?"

Her face said it all.

"Really, Tucker?" She replied with great disappointment. "You can get a clerk for that," Landowski quipped, turning her attention away from her heartthrob. Moore did her best to stifle a grin. Tucker shot her the look and then looked for someone more responsive.

"Butler, hey, can I get some help over here?"

Butler was a clerk, much lower on the office totem pole than a fellow detective.

"Sure boss, what's up," Butler asked, making his way over to his superior.

"We've got a situation in interrogation one. Will you help me out?"

"No problem," Butler replied.

Tucker turned his attention to Moore.

"Meet me in room two. I'll get Paco."

Moore was relieved. Had she returned to that room, with the smells that could remain, it wouldn't have been a pretty picture. Moore made her way to room two and waited for the others to arrive.

Tucker followed Butler into the room with Paco, who looked much paler than when he first arrived.

"Are you done," Tucker asked before grabbing him up.

"Si," Paco replied. "But I ain't feelin' well." He was slow getting to his feet. "Can I get a Sprite or something?"

Butler answered before Tucker could ask.

"I'll bring one in room two."

Tucker nodded his thanks and removed Paco from the room. They walked down the hallway and into room two. Tucker pushed Paco down into the seat. After closing the door, Tucker resumed his posture in the corner. Moore looked at Paco who still looked like, any minute, he would blow another gasket. She decided this interview would be quick.

"Do you know anything about the murders, Miquel?"

"No."

"Did anybody have a grudge against Fred or Thelma?"

"Not that I know," Paco answered.

"Did they have debts? Did they owe you any money?"

Paco hesitated before responding. He may not have been feeling well, but he wasn't stupid. He knew the fast circular questions was the officer's way of hooking him into this situation.

"This ain't about no drugs," Paco began.

Tucker perked up, and Moore leaned in.

"What do you know, Paco," Tucker asked sternly.

"I know you're barking up the, how do you say, the wrong tree."

"Okay, then what tree should we be barking up," Moore inquired.

"I don't want to get involved," Paco offered.

"Too late for that, Miquel. Either you tell us, or we'll make sure you're involved."

That wasn't a veiled threat. Paco had a long track record of misdemeanor crimes. All it would take was one misstep, and he knew they could hem him up for any number of things. No judge in three counties would believe he was innocent of anything he was accused of, whether it was true or not. Paco's head was pounding. He needed to get out of the police station so he could get his fix. The longer he stayed, the sicker he knew he would be.

"Listen, check the kids."

Tucker looked at Moore. She took the lead.

"Mimi's dead, Paco."

"That ain't Fred's kid."

"Then who are you talking about and make it plain," Moore insisted.

"Look at the kids they got paid for." Paco dropped his head into his hands. The pounding was relentless.

"Anyone in particular?"

"All them kids had a reason to hate Thelma, Fred, too."

"Anything else you can tell us, Paco?"

"No, nada, that's all I know. Now, can I go?"

"Sure Paco, but don't go far," Tucker warned. "We may need to talk to you again."

Paco nodded his head and eye-checked with the officers before getting up. Butler was just coming into the office with the soda that was requested.

"Butler, would you get him home?" Moore asked.

"Sure."

Butler handed Paco the soda, and the two left down the hall. Tucker and Moore put their heads together.

"We need that response back from the state. I don't know how many kids they had in their home, but that would give us some place to start."

Chapter Eleven

Before leaving the restaurant, Chloe bought several meals. She couldn't bear to go back to the underpass empty handed. The ride back with Stanley was much more interactive than before. He shared more of himself with them and made himself available if they needed to speak with him again. That was a big step for Mr. Lucas, but he was okay with it. He wanted that murderous lady off the street, and if that meant compromising his own anonymity, then he was willing to do that. Once they returned Professor Lucas to his locale and gave him some extra food to get through the evening, Michael wheeled the SUV back to the other side where Chloe saw the small child.

"They may not be here," Michael offered.

"I know, but I have to try," Chloe replied.

Once again, the two struck out with flashlights in hand. Michael held the bags of food as they walked the underpass. There were more people on the slant than before; out from under the eaves.

Maybe it was the time of day, Michael and Chloe were not sure. As they met the various individuals, Chloe handed out the food, all the while, looking for the child she saw earlier. They were just about to the end of the provisions when a woman with a small child moved down the embankment. Michael held the flashlight low. He didn't want to make the same mistake they made before. The two waited until the mom and child approached, not wanting to frighten them off.

The mother looked relatively young. The boy stood behind her leg, not wanting to approach the strangers. All of this was heartbreaking for Dr. Daniels. There was no conversation necessary, though. Chloe extended the food, and the mom reached out to accept it. The child never made his or her face clear, but as soon as the mom received the food, she thanked the two and moved away. Chloe wasn't sure if that was the child she initially saw in the eaves of the overpass, but it was a child, nonetheless. When all the food was gone, Michael and Chloe returned to the SUV. Chloe's face was even more somber than it had been the first time. The break they got in the case seemed to pale in comparison to her experience with the homeless.

Michael drove in silence. The day had been exceptionally long. They both were tired.

"It's not enough," Chloe said. She was still looking out of the passenger window, but Michael heard her.

"I know, but it's something," he replied, trying to sound hopeful.

Chloe appreciated what Michael said. Still, she was saddened by the totality of the situation.

A crack in the police radio broke the silence.

"We've got a 246, active shooter at Devereux Youth Center. All officers in the area need to respond. That's a 246 at Devereux."

Chloe looked over to Michael.

"You need to go," she asked.

Before he could respond, his cell phone rang.

"I need you out there."

It was Chief Livingston.

"I'm downtown. I've got Dr. Daniels with me," Detective Phillips replied.

"Bring her with you. We need all hands on deck, and there's no time for drop offs. I'll meet you there."

It wasn't a request; it was a command. Although Chloe only heard Michael's end of the conversation, she could tell by his posture, who was on the other end of the phone. When the line disconnected, Michael started to explain.

"Don't bother. Let's go."

Attorney Ethan Ross had been ordered to meet with Anna Black one more time before the trial. To say Ross did so begrudgingly was an understatement. He had no desire to ever speak with inmate Black again, but his boss gave him little option.

Because the trial was scheduled for the next couple of days, inmate Black was being held at the Fulton County Jail. Needless to say, her presence in the local community was not well received by either the community or the prison population. Attorney Ross expected to and did have to wade through hordes of media and demonstrators as he made his way into the jail. Some of the signs the protestors carried he did find interesting. They didn't hold back in their sentiments regarding Anna Black. That was the highlight of Ross' adventure.

Once inside the room where he was scheduled to meet with the inmate, Ross fumbled through his briefcase to find the witness list and the plan of attack he prepared while he was still her attorney. His boss was hoping inmate Black would have a change of heart and allow the Public Defender's office to represent her once again. If this thing went south with Anna representing herself, the public defender's office wanted to be able to say they put forth every effort on behalf of one of their most famous clients. Was it a political move? Absolutely, and Ross was aware of the role he played in it.

It didn't take long before inmate Black was taken out of her cell in solitary confinement and walked down to meet with the attorney. This was the opportunity the other prisoners waited for. The vulgar signs the protestors held outside the jail walls didn't compare to the litany of vulgarities slung at Anna as the two guards paraded her in front of her peers.

"Bitch, you betta hope they don't send your ass back here after court!"

"I'll kill you myself, Black! You ain't shit!"

"They gone fry yo white ass!"

"You ain't tough, trick! Let them guards let you loose up in this piece! We'll take care of yo cracker ass!"

Anna was oblivious to the hurtful words directed at her. She greeted the sneers and jeers with an unwavering smile which only incited the prisoners more. The guards attempted to quell the fray, but their voices went unheard over the whoops and hollers about Anna Black.

Amongst all the cat calls were a few, who admired Anna's work. Why wouldn't they? Anna Black was a legend in her own time; a female serial killer.

"Anna Black! You my girl!"

"Love you, Anna!"

"Anna, will you be my angel?"

Despite what they said, whether positive or negative, inmate Black returned the same plastered on smile. It was only when the guards guided her down the hallway where the meeting room was did things quiet down. You could still hear the inmates going off in the background, but it was much quieter as the guards moved further away.

Attorney Ross heard the ruckus outside the door and knew his ex-client was en route. Not long after, the door opened, and inmate Anna Black was walked into the room. Ross indicated his desire for the guards to remain in the room. He refused to be alone with Anna if he could help it. She unnerved him, and if she tried anything, he didn't want to have to call anyone for assistance. After the guards chained the inmate to the chair, by hands and feet, they resigned themselves to the background.

"I fired you," Anna lit in immediately. "What are you doing here?"

"Nice to see you too, Ms. Black."

"Quit with the formalities and answer the question." Anna was very no nonsense.

"Trust me," Ross retorted, "if I had my way, I wouldn't be here. So let's try and make this as quick and painless as possible. Shall we?"

Anna should have been glad to finally have someone to talk to. There was no one she could confer with in solitary. Not even the guards would talk to her. But Anna didn't like Ross, and she made that perfectly clear.

"What can I do for you, Attorney Ross?"

Just like that, Anna's disposition flipped. She smiled at him in a way that made his skin crawl.

"Do you still intend to represent yourself in court?"

"I sure do."

"Have you given any thought to rehiring the public defenders' office, so you have proper legal representation?"

"No, I have not."

"Did you listen to the warnings Judge Bledsoe issued? If you think that somehow you will get off on appeal because you represent yourself, chances of that are slim," Ross cautioned.

"That's why I fired you in the first place," Anna shot back.

"What are you talking about?"

"Didn't you hear what you just said, Attorney Ross? Do you think about the things you say before you say them?"

Ross was still perplexed by her statement. Anna saw his confusion and proceeded to clarify.

"You said, if I think I can get an appeal, did you not?"

"Yes, I did, but..."

Anna cut him off before he could continue.

"You presume, Attorney Ross, that I am guilty. In order to try for an appeal you must first be found guilty. Is that right, Attorney Ross?"

"Well, yeah." Ethan realized the error in his argument. So did the guards in the room who shot a look at each other.

"What I mean is..."

Once again, Ross was interrupted.

"How then can I have the best possible representation if my own attorney thinks I'm guilty?"

Ross didn't even try to respond. The room was uncomfortably quiet for a few moments.

"Listen, Ms. Black," he began much more humbly. "All I'm saying is, the prosecutor has a whole litany of witnesses to testify against you. Eyewitnesses who saw you with syringes in your hands. The prosecutor has forensic evidence, medical reports, psychological reports... a mountain of evidence against you."

"I'm sure she does, Attorney Ross," Anna replied unbothered. "You know the one thing I have that she doesn't?"

"What's that," Ross asked.

"The truth, Attorney Ross," Anna said proudly. "I have the undoctored, unadulterated truth on my side. So I don't care if that prosecutor parades 100 witnesses in front of the jury. I don't care if she has piles and piles of evidence. As a matter of fact, I don't care what any of them say. They don't have what I have. I've got the truth on my side, and that's enough."

"But it's not enough," Ross replied, attempting to reason with the inmate. "Beyond a reasonable doubt is the benchmark in a case like this. Beyond a reasonable doubt. Don't you think with all of the evidence the prosecutor's office has that most reasonable people would believe what she has over what you say?"

Anna didn't need time to ponder his question.

"Any reasonable person, Attorney Ross, will believe the truth."

Ethan's exacerbation was beginning to show. He didn't know what else to say to Anna. She was unreachable as far as he was concerned. Ross decided to give it one last ditch effort so he could go back to his boss and say he tried everything he knew how.

"Ms. Black, please consider having an attorney of some sort. Can you afford to hire an attorney if you don't want a representative from my office?"

"I refuse to pay for what I'm entitled to."

"So is that a no?"

"That's a, 'I refuse to pay for what I'm entitled to'."

"Is there anything I can say to convince you that you need a licensed legal attorney to represent you, or at least sit with you in court, just in case you get stuck on a legal precedent or something?"

This was the first time Anna paused and considered what the attorney had to say. Anna took her time thinking about it before responding.

"If, and I do mean if, I decide that I am open to having an attorney sit with me, will said attorney agree to speak only when I ask for help or defer to him or her?"

"I don't think that would be a problem," Ross replied.

"And if, and again, I'm stressing the if part, if I agree to have an attorney from your office present, would they agree to follow my lead and not try to over talk me or respond to the judge without referring back to me as the primary attorney in my own case?"

"I'm sure that can be arranged."

Ross wasn't sure, but he would rather go back to his boss with something rather than nothing; even if it was unreasonable.

"And if I agree to having a representative from the public defender's office as my second chair, will that person truly believe in my innocence?"

That was the statement that gave Ross pause. He couldn't think of anyone in his office who didn't believe Anna Black was guilty as sin. However, it wasn't his decision to make. He would leave that call to those on a higher pay grade than he was.

"I'm sure we can arrange that."

"Well, in that case, Attorney Ross, go tell your superiors that if they meet all the requirements as I have stated to you, then a representative can be present as my second chair."

"Excellent Ms. Black. I will certainly relay your message."

Good then," Anna replied. "I would shake your hand to confirm our agreement but considering the chains..."

"I understand."

The guards took their cue and loosened Anna's restraints so she could be transported back to her cell. Ethan was glad the conversation was over. He could hardly wait to get back to his office and relay Anna Black's demands.

Logan was good with his clients, and he knew it. He didn't take being a physical trainer lightly. When Logan decided to journey towards health and wellness, he didn't take any shortcuts. Logan studied, took courses, and was certified in a variety of components as a trainer. Logan's business was thriving. His waiting list grew, and most of the women he worked with wanted more from him than he was willing to give. It goes without saying that Logan's popularity did not always sit well with the other trainers. That was just par for the course in Logan's estimation. It was his disarming charm and magnanimous personality that kept things cordial with the other trainers, even though he was stealing their clients.

Logan had an unfair advantage over the other trainers, though. Something he learned when he was battling the fat kid he continued to see in the mirror. Logan went through years of counseling and therapy; first at his parents' behest. Logan was an identical twin. His twin brother, Landon, didn't struggle with childhood obesity like Logan did.

Their parents, Olivia and Charles, couldn't understand what happened; why the two progressed so differently. The Spencer's had a track record of being excellent parents as evidenced by the twins' older sister, Dakota. She, like Landon, was healthy, fit, athletic and popular. How Logan failed, of course, was troubling to them.

And for type A personality, fairly well off white folks, psychotherapy was the answer to all their problems. Being in counseling for one issue or another was almost a status symbol. There was no shame in it, unless you were going for a reason you could not control, and your parents thought you to be the consummate failure. So Logan didn't appreciate having to sit in front of some stranger and explain why he failed at maintaining a healthy body weight when his twin, well, all his family members were active, appropriately weighted individuals. He didn't relish in it at all. However, there was a benefit Logan gained that he eventually mastered. The therapist used neurolinguistic programming to suggest behavior without overtly suggesting behavioral change. Neurolinguistic programming is the art of leading touch and word association to get people to do what you want them to do. More than that, the controlled individual willfully complies without knowledge of the influencing factor.

What the other trainers, even Logan's clients didn't know, is that he used this kind of mental control to have his own needs met. They were lambs to his slaughter; yet, his hands remained clean. That's how Logan liked it... clean.

Chapter Twelve

Sitting in front of her sewing machine, Grace was incredibly frustrated. Things were not going according to any of her most recent plans, and her husband had gotten completely beside himself. Drake never spoke to her that way before, and the fact he felt he could without repercussion, sent Grace to a place she wasn't sure she could come back from. The house was quiet, too damn quiet. Grace didn't have any friend girls she wanted to be bothered with. They were all fake and phony anyway.

Finding her way to her husband's bar, Grace poured herself a hefty drink, and then another; and before it was all over, she poured one more. The only thing that seemed to soothe her, here of late, was putting together her next costume. The new shipment of patent leather shoes came in the other morning. She worked on the lace socks late last night. But the satisfaction she felt from that was short-lived. Grace knew, more than anything else, she needed another girl; just one more. Maybe if she had a replacement, all the bad feelings she was having would go away. The problem though was Drake. He was on to her. He knew way too much to let her get away with what she'd gotten away with in the past. Grace wasn't one for going out into the real world, finding a girl, and executing her in the street. That wasn't her style. She much preferred the comfort of her own home where she had the upper hand.

Grace continued to sip the dark liquor from her glass as she considered what to do to satisfy her seemingly insatiable appetite. She was more than a little tipsy now. When her glass was near empty, Grace ventured out once again for a refill. Swaying from one side of the hallway to the other, Grace felt pretty damn good. When she misfired on her glass when pouring the expensive bourbon, she had to keep herself from giggling.

"Whoaaaa..."

She snorted, which was completely undignified, and then snickered for doing so. Her return to her office space was just as zig-zagging as the trot down. Grace overshot her swivel chair and nearly fell to the floor. Now, she was laughing full on as she tried to save the drink from spilling.

"Oh, my!" Grace bellowed, tempered with fits of laughter. She was able to right herself in the chair and preserve her drink, which was the most important part.

"Gracie, you bad, bad girl," she spoke into the atmosphere. Hearing her own voice, slurred speech and all, against nothing but quiet tickled Grace. It was also sobering. Drake called her Gracie; only when he was being a smart ass, mimicking the father, she loved so much. Thinking about Old Man Pembroke was sobering, as thoughts of Miriam were always tied to him. Grace sipped and recalled.

She never liked to travel down this train of thought. It was far too painful; peppered with anger and mistrust. Her father never wanted to discuss why he sent Miriam away no matter how much young Grace pressed him. He talked bad about Miriam; called her worthless, and always managed to skirt the question his only daughter raised. But Grace had memories of her own; memories blockaded by years of deceit and deception, and plain dishonesty by the man she loved more than all the world. There was a bit of deception by Miriam, as well.

Grace found herself nodding off. Envisioning a potential crash with the floor, she decided to move to the family room where she could stretch out.

There was a bottle of bourbon there too, and she topped off her glass before curling up on the couch.

"Bottoms up," Grace announced; air toasting her drink. She pinched her nose tight and guzzled the lukewarm liquid. It burned nicely as it traveled down her throat and settled in her empty belly. Before long, Grace was fully engulfed by the demons of her past.

Grace was young, far too young to actually understand what she witnessed. And of course, it was explained away by her father. That Grace learned to live with. She knew her father sometimes had to lie to protect her. He did it because he loved her. That was excusable, right?

But some things you just can't unsee, no matter how many lies the adults in your life tell you. Flashes came to her from her youth; flashes of things she'd seen before. Grace nestled in on the couch. The empty glass fell to the carpeted floor. Deeper sleep overtook her, and quickly settled where dreams come in. But this was more than a dream for Grace. She remembered; stolen glances and guilty faces. Grace remembered her father lingering when Miriam was around; staying when there was no reason for him to. He claimed to despise all Black folks, but Grace clearly remembered him touching Miriam as though he cared. And when Grace saw Old Man Pembroke, being gentle with the help, he chastised Miriam mercilessly. Her father didn't do that with the other servants. He was never nice to them.

Even in her sleep, Grace's face contorted as the unpleasantness she closeted off resurfaced. She remembered. It was late. There was a storm, a massive storm. Trees surrounding the Pembroke mansion bent under the unrelenting wind and rain. It howled, like a lone wolf, shaking young Grace from slumber. Grabbing her baby doll and holding it close, Grace cowered under the covers. And then the rumbling started; low and then louder, shaking the very foundation of her beloved home. Young Grace's body shook nearly as much as the house. It was a great distance between her bedroom and that of her father's. Grace couldn't decide whether it was scarier to stay where she was or risk the long hallway to get to her dad.

The sky outside her window lit up. Long shadows were cast across Grace's room. They were frightening, and she hunkered down even lower in the cover, nearly covering her head. She wanted to see but was afraid to look. The storm was unrelenting. The wind and rain beat steadily against the tall pane windows, and the grumble of thunder was getting to be too much for little

Gracie. Her father taught her to be strong and fearless. He didn't want a weakling for a daughter. He already had one for a wife, and Old Man Pembroke wouldn't stand to see that duplicated in his only child. So Grace was brave in weathering the storm; as brave as any little girl could be.

And then it all happened at once. Seemingly simultaneous booms, and cracks and blasts of bright light and something hard and violent smacked against her window. It was too much! Grace leaped from her bed and braved the hallway, clinging to her doll for comfort. It was polite to knock. Grace was taught to be polite. But fear trumped politeness and Grace bolted into her father's bedroom unannounced. Grace was tall enough to see over the side of the bed.

"Da-

The scream of her father's name stopped short in her throat, and the faces that returned in her direction stopped Grace's feet from moving.

He was angry, and she was ashamed. Old Man Pembroke didn't wait to chastise her.

"You didn't lock the door?"

"I'm sor-

He addressed the blackness in his bed with a backhand to the face before returning what he deemed a much softer gaze in his daughter's direction.

"Was it the storm, Gracie," Pembroke asked, climbing down from the four poster bed. But not before Grace saw the face of the one he slapped. Confused, Grace couldn't respond to her father. He was already at her side, turning her away from his adulterous bed before what she saw struck her dumb. As they passed the door's threshold, she heard a naked Miriam whimper. Grace tossed on the couch, uncomfortable with the imagery.

The next day, Miriam was sent away. There was no explanation given. Old Man Pembroke decided an explanation was not necessary. The memory of Miriam walking in slow motion down the main hallway, opening the bigger than life front door, and descending so gracefully down the front stairs, even in her shame haunted Grace, now, in her daymare. Even in her adult sleep, Grace whimpered for the one she lost.

Devereux was nearly an hour from where Dr. Daniels and Phillips were located. Michael had not debriefed Chloe, but whatever it was, the full force of the Atlanta Police Department was needed. Devereux was not in APD's catchment area. But something about this situation erased geographical districting lines. The big brass made the decision that Phillips should be there and that's what he was going to do. Kennesaw, where Devereux was located, was a boujie suburban area. Their police force typically dealt with retail and residential burglaries as high priority cases. This was murder. They needed all the help they could get.

Chloe was totally consumed in her own thoughts, even with the pressure of this new situation on the horizon. Michael briefly visually checked in with Chloe, seeing the distance in her eyes.

"Do you want to talk about it?" He asked as he expertly navigated his truck through traffic.

Her hesitation was slight before Chloe sighed. Her heart was heavy.

"We have to go back to them," she began, still looking waywardly out of the window. "Not now, but we have to go back, Michael."

"Whenever you're ready," he replied. Although Michael saw it more than Chloe did, being up close and personal with the homeless situation resonated with him, too.

"I just can't get those kids off my mind…"

Chloe's voice trailed off. Michael couldn't see she was fighting back the tears, but he heard genuine concern in her voice. Michael moved the SUV along in an open stretch of highway. The sun was starting to set, and the roadway was dotted with headlights casting short range illumination against the setting suns' orange glow.

"I feel so damn helpless," Chloe continued.

Her statement caught Michael's attention; of course with the gravity of the words she spoke, but more because Chloe was not known to curse. His slight smile felt inappropriate considering the situation, and so it dissolved as quickly as it appeared.

"I promise, we will go back," Michael replied reassuringly.

That satisfied Chloe temporarily. She knew Michael to be a man of his word. The beep of her cell phone drew Chloe's attention away from her current dilemma.

Good evening. I was hoping we would have a chance to discuss the case before court on Wednesday. Waiting for your call.

Chloe couldn't help rolling her eyes. Almost as soon as she'd done it, Chloe regretted involving Nigel in her business matters. He wouldn't let it just be that. He always wanted more. Chloe refused to respond to his text. Maybe she would deal with it later, maybe not. Swirls of colors quickly changed Chloe's focus. Chloe sent a quick text to Addison to let her know where she was headed. After that, Dr. Daniels dropped her cell phone in her jacket pocket and didn't think about it anymore.

With red and blue lights blazing, siren blaring and the HOV lane, Detective Phillips shaved off significant time on the trip. The way the Chief sounded on the phone let Michael know this was no time to mess around. Even before Michaels' SUV pulled up to the facility, a strong police presence was not only seen but felt. Streets two blocks over were barricaded. Traffic was rerouted. Helicopters with spotlights capable of pinpointing suspects in utter darkness circled overhead. Michael slowed the truck to a crawl, looking for a place to pull over.

Major knew when he offed that kid, he was bringing heat to their situation. The blast from his gun brought all the people to the yard. Major and Mayven had to think quick. Major made his way back to her.

"Run or stay," Mayven asked.

She trusted Major implicitly. If he decided to run, she would go with him without question. If he decided they should stay, then that's exactly what they would do. The pact between the two was deeper than the superficial. They had a blood pact.

Major didn't respond.

She looked into Major's eyes. His indecisiveness in the moment was concerning. Major didn't answer because he was considering Mayven. He didn't say that, but he didn't ever want anything else bad to happen to her. She'd been through too much already. He was concerned and quiet. Mayven saw uncertainty. In that moment, she made the decision for both of them.

"Hostages... leverage..."

That was it. The decision was made. The two backpedaled into Brigadoon. Major would protect her with his life. That, he was committed to. Brigadoon's residents watched the whole thing from the windows, and even a few of the young men stood in the doorway. When they saw the culprits coming back, they turned tail and scattered. It was cool when the aggression targeted staff. Seeing one of their counterparts gunned down? That was different.

Once safely inside the house, Major moved to barricade the front door. Pushing the chairs aside, Major pulled the heavy wood dining room table to block the entrance. The doors automatically locked from the inside and required a key for entry. The barricade was as much a psychological measure as one more impediment to anyone who breached the threshold. Satisfied with the security of the front door, Major moved to the back and found heavy objects to block it as well. In the meantime, Mayven checked all the windows to make sure they were securely locked. The two met back up in the office when they were done.

"They need to know who they dealing with," Major explained to Mayven. With that, the two moved systematically through the residence hall. The kids would be their greatest leverage. Those that were not in their bedrooms were placed in one, directly in front of the window with the curtains pulled back.

"Touch the window, I'll kill you. Scream? I'll kill you. Move? I will kill you."

Major gave the warning to each of the remaining residents. He pointed the gun at their head to ensure they knew he wasn't playing around.

Familiarity breeds contempt, and Major didn't want the youngsters getting too comfortable with them. They weren't here to make friends. They came to Devereux to prove a point. Walking out of the last residents' room, Major checked in with Mayven.

163

"That's ten," he shouted.

Mayven stopped what she was doing and met Major in the hallway.

"There's one missing."

There should be twelve. With the one dead in the yard, Major should have rounded up eleven. There was one unaccounted for. The two spread out, Mayven going one way and Major going the other. They scoured the building in search of the one that was missing.

Outside, things were heating up. It looked as if the media was notified almost as soon as the police were made aware of what was going on. They were out in full force, and their bright lights and flashing cameras had the area lit up like a movie set. After parking, Detective Phillips and Dr. Daniels made their way to the makeshift command center positioned near the guard shack on the facility's property. Chief Livingston was there barking orders to anyone within hearing distance. When he spotted Phillips and Daniels, he waved them over.

"I need bodies, around the perimeter. Do not breach the grounds until you hear from me! Is that clear?" Chief Livingston barked into the walkie talkie. He received several replies of clear on the other end. "And keep the motherfuckin' media back!"

"Chief," Phillips addressed, as the two approached the table Livingston was leaning on. "What do we have?"

"That's part of the problem," Chief Livingston began. His brow had more lines in it than Dr. Daniels ever noticed before. Clearly, he was frustrated by the situation. "We have very little Intel coming from inside the facility, and when I say very little, I mean just that."

"What do we know?" Phillips prodded, trying to help the Chief focus on the facts. With the big brass looking for immediate rectification of the situation, several officers vying for his attention, and the media encroaching on the perimeter the police established, Livingston felt the pressure.

"From our copter overhead, we have one body near the resident's houses in the back of the property." Livingston drew their attention to a Devereux brochure typically used with visitors that earmarked the property's layout. Both Phillips and Daniels leaned in.

"It looks like there are six houses back there. We don't know how many assailants there are. I have spoken with the director of the facility. She advised there are at least 72 residents, well 71 residents between the six houses. We don't know if one of the kids did it or whether it was someone from the outside."

"Is anyone checking vehicle tags," Daniels asked. Both of the men looked up. "I was just thinking, that may be a way of telling what cars belong on the property and which one's don't."

Chief Livingston hit the button on the walkie-talkie. "Christian, see if we can get a list of the cars and plates coming through security in the past twelve hours. Determine whether they have video surveillance or a log."

That was Daniels confirmation that the Chief liked her idea. He wouldn't thank her overtly, but his quick action said it all.

"Christian's back at headquarters?" Phillips clarified.

"Yeah, I needed someone to coordinate logistics and a central line for call-throughs, while I run point."

"Good idea," Phillips offered. "I don't know Chief," Phillips continued. "For all we know, one of the staff people could have done it."

"Exactly, Phillips," Livingston concurred. "See the problem?"

Chapter Thirteen

Her head was foggy, and it hurt. Her eyes felt heavy; weighted down in their sockets. Slowly, she peeled them open. The bright light of the room assaulted her vision, and she quickly shut them again. The rancid taste in her mouth was a horrible reminder of what she'd done. The stale bourbon reminded her of Drake, most nights. Grace didn't know how long she'd been asleep on the couch. She wished she didn't remember what assaulted her dreams, but she did.

Uncurling from the couch, Grace opened her eyes to a slit and stood up.

"Mmph," she moaned, as her foot stepped on the tail of the fallen wine glass. Fortunately, it didn't break, but the change in surface was enough to get her attention. Grace's eyes were forced open, sufficient enough to navigate to the powder room. Every step was dizzying. But Grace made it and held her balance with the assistance of the porcelain sink. Even before she looked into the mirror, she opened the vanity and pulled out mouthwash, toothpaste and a toothbrush. Loading the brush, Grace vigorously brushed her teeth, fighting off the foul taste. Once done, she rinsed the brush under the running water and unscrewed the cap on the travel size mouthwash initially placed in the bathroom for guests, i.e., the help, who never got the chance to use it.

Grace threw the mouthwash back, filling her mouth to capacity. She started to gargle, and the sound made her laugh; opening her airway enough for the blue-tinged liquid to choke her. Now, Grace braced herself at the lip of the porcelain toilet, as the contents of her belly forcefully emptied out. The stench wafted from the bowl and choked Grace even more. Her stomach contents were gone. All that was left was bile, and she gagged and vomited until her eyes bulged, and tears ran down her cheeks. Intoxication also loosened her sphincter control, and the pompous Grace Pembroke Wetherby shit her pants.

"UGH!"

The putrid taste in her mouth and the horrid odor from Grace's bony ass, converged in the confines of the powder room. Grace felt unwelcomed moisture staining her granny panties and the back of her slacks. She was so disgusted with herself, all she could do was brace herself against the closest wall with her ass lifted so as to not spread the nastiness.

"This is so ridiculous," Grace began with self-chastisement.

"If my friends could see me now!" Grace yelled out. "Snooty bitches!"

That tickled Grace's fancy, and she started to giggle. That quickly turned into boisterous laughter that echoed down the hallway. The bounce back from the cavernous hall tickled Grace even more, and soon she was doubled up on the floor embracing her empty belly. And then she farted. Grace howled with laughter that simultaneously wafted with the smell. Drunk or not, Grace laughed until it hurt.

After a while, she peeled herself from the floor. She was still a bit wobbly on her feet. Finally flushing the contaminated toilet, Grace made her way out of the powder room. Her walk was awkward as the mess in her panties moved with her. The walk to the master bathroom seemed longer than usual, but Grace finally stumbled in, leaving a trail of malodorous leavings behind her. She undressed, leaving her soiled clothes in a pile on the floor and stepped in the shower before turning on the water. As Grace twisted the stainless steel knob, icy water jetted from the shower head.

"MOTHERFUCKER!"

She squealed as she leaped to avoid the multiple trails of frosty droplets. Whatever remnants of drunkenness that may have lingered were shocked from Grace's system. By the time the water warmed sufficiently, Mrs. Wetherby was sober. Grace allowed the now steamy water to rinse her from head to toe. She took special care to clean in areas she personally contaminated. After she was done, Grace felt much better. Wrapping herself in a plush towel, Grace made her way to the basin to brush her teeth. This time, she decided mouthwash wasn't necessary.

Finding clothes sufficient enough to wear around the house, Grace restarted where she'd left off, in her sewing room. This time, though, her agenda was clear. Grace found her phonebook. The name she was looking for was very specific. Picking up the phone sitting near her sewing machine, Grace dialed the number.

"Hello?"

"May I speak with Carmen Moore?"

"This is Carmen. Who's calling?

"Hi Carmen, This is Mrs. Wetherby."

The other end of the line fell deadly silent.

"Carmen, are you still there?"

"Yes, Mrs. Wetherby. I'm here." Carmen was taken aback by the call and the overly friendly nature in which Grace spoke.

"I was wondering if you were still looking for employment."

"Why?"

The inquiry and the intonation caught Grace off guard. *Insolent bitch.*

"Well, Carmen, if you must know, our last girl, I mean nanny, didn't work out. So, I was wondering if you would consider coming to work with us?"

Silence greeted Grace again. She would have thought the likes of Carmen Moore would have jumped at such an opportunity.

"Well, Mrs. Wetherby, I am no longer available."

"Why may I ask?"

"Of course you can ask," Carmen gloated.

"Your husband, Mr. Wetherby, gave me a lead with another family and I have been happily working with them ever since."

Traitorous bastard, Grace thought to herself.

"You seem awfully happy?"

"I am," Carmen replied confidently.

"Well Ms. Moore," Grace began.

"Mrs.," Carmen corrected.

"Excuse me, Mrs. Moore," Grace replied, rolling her eyes. "Whatever the family is paying you, I will double it. And if you start this week, I will give you a $1,000 signing bonus."

Now the silence on the other end was expected by Grace. Carmen didn't know what to say. Her family could certainly use the money but to subject herself to Mrs. Wetherby? Carmen wasn't convinced the money was worth it.

"I will get back with you."

Grace was shocked the bitch didn't leap at such a generous offer, but she played it cool. She didn't want to run her away with an oversell.

"Certainly, Mrs. Moore. However, please make a decision as quickly as possible. We desperately need someone and my children can't stop talking about you."

No, she didn't throw the children in it, Carmen scoffed.

"Absolutely," Carmen replied. "I will let you know one way or the other in the next day or so."

"Perfect," Grace bubbled. "Talk to you soon, Carmen."

"Goodbye, Mrs. Wetherby."

This time Grace waited until Carmen disconnected the line. She wouldn't want the help to think her rude. When she heard the definitive sound of the call ending, Grace hung up her phone and placed it back in its cradle.

The prospect of having a new girl made Grace giddy.

"She'll accept my offer," Grace mused. "I know she will."

Carmen gripped the cell phone in her hand long after the call ended. She kept looking at the phone in disbelief. The odd look on her face is what drew her husband's attention as he sat next to her on the couch.

"What's up?" Jermaine asked; his attention split between his wife and the basketball game on the television. "Did I hear you right?"

"If you heard me say, Mrs. Wetherby, yeah, you heard right."

"What the hell does she want?" Jermaine asked, sitting on the edge of his seat as his team stormed toward the goal.

"Can you believe that bitch offered me a job?"

"Come on man! What's with all the bricks?" Jermaine scolded the television. Aggravated he slumped back on the couch and gave his wife a greater portion of his attention.

"Offered you a job? You got a job. Did you tell her that?"

"Yeah, I did," Carmen replied. "That's when she offered me a bonus."

Now Carmen had her husband's full attention. Grabbing the remote, Jermaine hit the mute button and fully turned towards his wife.

"She did what?" Jermaine asked perplexed.

"That crazy woman not only offered me a thousand dollar bonus, but she said if I came to work for her, she would double my salary." Carmen still couldn't believe it even as she repeated it.

"The hell?"

"Yeah, and she was serious, too."

"So what did you tell her," Jermaine asked.

"I told her I would get back to her. I needed to think about it."

"Think about what," Beatrice asked, entering the living room.

Carmen rolled her eyes. Living with her mom, she and Jermaine didn't have any privacy to speak of.

"It's nothing Ma," Carmen answered.

"It must be something if your husband over there tore himself away from that stupid basketball game."

Beatrice made herself comfortable on the couch across from the couple. She crossed her legs and waited for an answer.

"We'll talk about it later," Carmen leaned over and said to Jermaine.

"Huh, don't mind me," Beatrice suggested. "I ain't trying to be in your little business no way."

"But you are Ma; you are in our business."

"And you in my house!"

No matter how much of an adult Carmen was, her mother had a way of reducing her to child status.

Jermaine did his best to stay out of it, looking at the TV screen feigning interest in the muted game.

The trio was silent. Beatrice, with her arms folded across her ample chest, glared at her daughter.

"You are seriously not going to tell me? If it impacts you Carmen Marie, it impacts me."

"Really, Ma?"

"Really!"

The frustration Carmen felt grew exponentially every time she had to engage her nosey ass mother. She couldn't wait until she and her family had a place to call their own. That alone made the Wetherby offer much more attractive.

"Instead of wasting your time watching multi-millionaires running up and down the basketball court, you need to be looking for a job," Beatrice sniped at Jermaine.

He already knew it wouldn't be long before she dragged him into her rant.

"We are not going to start this again today," Carmen announced.

"Start what?" Beatrice responded playing innocent. "Encouraging your bum of a husband to get up off his lazy ass and get a job is not starting anything apparently."

This conversation Jermaine had no interest in joining. Getting up from the couch, he walked into their bedroom and closed the door. Carmen watched him as he exited.

"Why do you always have to do that?"

"I'm doing what you need to be doing," Beatrice shot back.

"Don't you think he feels bad enough? Your slick ass remarks don't help mom," Carmen quipped.

"I know you didn't just cuss at me?"

Again, reduced to child status.

"Well you ain't gone have to worry about us too much longer anyway so..."

"And why's that," Beatrice asked flippantly.

"Because as soon as we save up enough money, we are getting the hell out of here."

"Girl, at the rate things are going, Felicity will be in kindergarten before y'all get the hell out of here."

"That's what you think," Carmen snapped back.

"With that little bit of money you making working for them white folks, I think I'm right."

"Well, some more white folks offered me more money so...," Carmen snipped.

"What, two or three more dollars?"

"Double and a bonus, so like I said, you won't have to deal with us too much longer, mother."

Carmen went into the bedroom where her husband and daughter were. Jermaine was playing with little Felicity, and it made Carmen's heart swell. Carmen loved her small family, and she knew that as parents, they were both in agreement of wanting only the best for Felicity.

"Babe," Carmen said, interrupting daddy daughter time. Felicity cooed and giggled at her father making funny faces. When Jermaine looked up, Carmen was reminded why she fell in love with him in the first place.

"Wassup, babe?" Jermaine's eyes were bright, and his smile was warm.

"Have you thought about what we were discussing before we were so rudely interrupted by bewitched out there?"

"Yeah, I have," Jermaine replied with a laugh.

"So what do you think I should do?"

Jermaine adjusted Felicity in his arm, and she laid her head of curly locs on his chest.

"I want you to do whatever would be best for you."

"For us, don't you mean?"

"Happy wife, happy life, right?"

"Yeah, I guess so," Carmen answered.

"Just know Carmen, whatever you decide, I support you 100%. I am trying babe, I really am, with trying to get a job. But in the meantime, I'll do whatever it takes to hold you down." Jermaine continued, "Since I'm not working right now, it's unfair for me to say what your working situation should be. I'll let you decide, and then we'll go from there."

Carmen paused and considered what Jermaine said. "I'll call that ole bat in the morning!"

Chapter Fourteen

Tension on the Devereux campus continued to escalate. As staff and leadership learned of what transpired, they made their way to the facility. As news of the death of one of the residents hit the news waves, parents and social workers flooded the phone lines trying to find out if the kid that was killed belonged to them. Everyone was growing more and more frightened and more and more agitated because the answers were not coming fast enough.

"We are right down the street from the Devereux Treatment facility where we have learned that one of the residents there has lost his life. Details of what happened continue to be sketchy. What we know right now is that the child that lost his life was a boy. Emergency staff have been unable to enter the compound as no determination has been made as to who the assailants are and whether or not they are still on campus property. The situation has not been stabilized enough for anyone from the outside to go in. All reports received at this time have come from the residents who found the body. Police Chief Livingston is on site, and the police have the facility surrounded. As we get more information, we will interrupt your regularly scheduled programming to make sure you hear it here first. Reporting live from Kennesaw, outside the campus of Devereux Treatment Facility, this is Gerald Ingram, Channel 5 news."

Every time the news broke in, phone calls and panic increased. Chief Livingston had his hands full. They were operating on bare bones intelligence.

"What you doing back here?"

The young man looked up from the floor of the closet where he hid. His eyes bulged, and his cheeks were creased with tear stains.

"I don't wanna die," the young man whispered.

"Then you shouldn't have hid then," Mayven shot back.

"Please lady, don't kill me," the young man sobbed, begging for his life.

"Ain't nobody gone kill you as long as you do what we say, okay?"

"Promise?"

"Yeah, promise. Now get yo ass up."

Mayven reached down and yanked the young man to his feet. Initially he pulled away from her, but reconsidered when the grip on his arm got tighter.

"What's your name, lil' man?"

"Ssshawn," he stammered. His body shook, he was so scared.

"Okay Shawn, take me to your bedroom."

"Please don't kill me!"

"Keep saying it, and Im'ma be tempted," Mayven said. "Now, which way is your room?"

Shawn's steps were halting as the two made their way from the closet in the back of the residence hall towards his bedroom.

"May, you got him?" Major called out from the front of the building.

"Yeah, I got him."

Making his way to where her voice came from, Major rounded the hall and saw the two walking towards him.

"This the lil' nigga that ran?" Major was still on ten. His emotions were all over the place.

"He cool, Bae, he cool," Mayven reassured.

Shawn's eyes got even bigger as Major made his way towards them.

"Please don't let him kill me, please," the young man begged.

"He ain't."

When Major reached the duo, he grabbed the young man's other arm and helped escort him into his identified bedroom. There was already a young man kneeling on the bed facing the window, as instructed.

"Get up there with him," Major demanded, shoving the young man in the intended direction.

Shawn stumbled badly. The young man already positioned at the window briefly looked over his shoulder. Seeing Major and Mayven in his doorway, he quickly turned back. He was scared, too.

Major walked up behind Shawn and waited until he got into position.

"Im'ma tell you like I told these other fools. If you holler, I'll kill you. If you leave this room without me or her telling you to, we both gone kill you. Got that?"

Shawn trembled as he nodded his head vigorously.

"Cool. Long as you do what we tell you, y'all gone be alright."

Both boys faced the window and didn't dare turn back around. Shawn felt a little better. At least he was not by himself.

Making their way back to the office, Major and Mayven strategized their next move.

"It ain't gone be long before the cops come up in here," Major offered.

"I know," Mayven replied. "So we don't let them back us into this corner."

"Okay baby girl, what you thinking?"

"Like I said before. We got leverage, baby. Them two up there is our ticket out of here."

"I like the way you think, girl," Major said smiling. "Bring yo fine ass here."

Mayven intentionally hesitated her step. Major reached out and grabbed her by the waist and pulled her into him. He leaned back against the hallway wall and Mayven went with him.

"I love you girl. You know that don't you?"

"No doubt."

They came together in a passionate kiss; their tongues dancing in perfect step. Mayven felt Major's nature rise as he pulled her tighter into him. As they disengaged, Mayven looked up into Major's steely eyes.

"Me and you?"

"Me and you."

The interview with Paco had not been as productive as Detective Moore would have liked. At the same time, at least they were able to rule Paco out as a suspect. They would interview him again, Fatima was sure, before this whole thing was over. Maybe there would be something he remembered that might prove helpful. One of her counterparts walked by the desk and dropped off a package. Moore was so busy combing over the details of the file that was building on the triple homicide, she scarcely looked up.

Briefly stopping to see what the package was, Fatima perked up when she saw the return address as the South Carolina Department of Family and Children Services. She did not address the envelope politely; quickly peeling back the seal and tearing open the top. Detective Moore started reading what looked to be a form letter.

Greetings Detective Fatima Moore;

The Department is in receipt of your correspondence requesting information on former foster parent Thelma Williams. Although we do not have a signed release of information from Ms. Williams giving expressed permission to disclose details regarding the children previously in her care, we are extending this professional courtesy as the Department understands the facts may be pertinent to a pending investigation.

The following names are of children that were in the home of Ms. Williams immediately before her foster license was terminated two years ago. We will not release the names of children under the age of 18 who are still in our care and custody. These are the names of the children who were there and are now considered legal adults. Admittedly, for the majority of the listed individuals, all we have is name and DOB. After aging out of our system, very little contact information is provided. If we have a last known address, same will be listed by the name.

Melanie Jones, 20, address unknown

Johnathan Beecher, 19, last known address Canton, Georgia

Jessica Palmer, 20, address unknown

Gerald Homer, 18, last known address Augusta, Georgia

Major Braggs, 20, last known address Atlanta, Georgia

Paul Brown, last known address Kitchings Mill, South Carolina

Leo Reddick, last known address Warrenville, South Carolina

Brian Gerardi, last known address Trenton, South Carolina

Lacey Lumpkin, last known address Belvedere, South Carolina

If you would like to make contact with Ms. Williams' licensing worker with regard to the children still in the care and custody of the department, you can reach Ms. Winona Hicks at 803-555-1400.

Detective Moore placed her elbows on her desk, not sure what to make of the list in front of her. There were more names than she thought would be on such a list for such a short period of time. What she couldn't determine from the information provided was the age of the kids while they were in the care of Ms. Williams, and how long they'd been gone before the home was shut down. The list provided Detective Moore with more questions than answers. Grabbing a notepad from her desk drawer, Fatima dialed the phone number for Ms. Hicks.

"It's a great day with Aiken County DFCAS, this is Winona Hicks, how may I serve you?"

Ms. Hicks sounded surprisingly upbeat.

"Ms. Hicks, this is Detective Moore from the Aiken Police Department."

"Yes, detective, how may I help you, today?"

"I am in receipt of the list of youth previously in the home of Ms. Thelma Williams, and I have a few questions."

"Oh, okay."

Detective Moore could detect a change in Ms. Hicks enthusiasm, but she pressed forward.

"It was just so terrible to hear about what happened to those poor people," Ms. Hicks replied. "I mean, just terrible."

"It was," Detective Moore replied, attempting to sound empathetic. Not that she wasn't, but empathy wasn't helping Fatima solve her case.

"That's why I am calling, Ms. Hicks," Detective Moore suggested.

"I understand. Anything the department can do to help we will certainly try."

"Is there any way you can tell me the last youth in her home before it was closed? That is what happened, right? The home was closed because of a violation?"

For the first time since the beginning of the call, Ms. Hicks was slow to respond.

"Well, yes," she started slowly. "We did end up closing the Williams' home."

"And may I ask why?"

There was a pause before Ms. Hicks spoke again. "Can you hold on just a second?"

"Sure," Detective Moore replied, speculating as to Ms. Hicks' hesitancy.

In an instant, the phone line went dead, and the silence was swiftly replaced by elevator music. Fatima doodled while she waited, playing tic tac toe with herself. When the line broke again, Fatima attended.

"Detective Moore?"

"Yes, Ms. Hicks?"

"Okay, just making sure you were still there. Sometimes this phone system acts all willy nilly, and we lose calls."

"No, I'm here," Fatima replied. She noticed how fast Ms. Hicks was speaking as if she was out of breath.

"Okay, so you wanted to know why the Williams foster home was closed."

"That's correct."

"Well, we found a couple of violations which were, unreported residents in the home, and there was an allegation of neglect that was substantiated. That in and of itself was sufficient grounds to terminate our contract with Ms. Williams, but you know how it is. We have lots of foster kids and not a lot of foster homes. But anyway, that's why we closed her home."

Detective Moore scribbled notes as she listened.

"You said, unreported residents?"

"Yes," Ms. Hicks replied. "One of our field agents conducted an unannounced home visit, and we learned that Ms. Williams' boyfriend was living there, as well as an adult daughter."

"Mr. Conners?"

"Yes, that's correct."

"And was the daughter, MiMi Williams?"

"Yes, that's also correct."

"So prior to this unannounced visit, the department had no knowledge that these adults lived in the home?"

There was another brief delay before Ms. Hicks replied.

"Being as Ms. Williams was a licensed foster parent with our agency, we were only required to complete one announced and one unannounced visit every six months. So, yes, this was the first time we had actual confirmation of the adults living there with the foster children in the home."

Detective Moore found that hard to believe, knowing what she knew about the family, but she didn't press. There was more she needed from Ms. Hicks, but she didn't want to offend her. However, as an investigator, Detective Moore just had to ask one more question.

"How were you able to confirm this time?"

"This is so embarrassing," Ms. Hicks began. "Our agent went out after business hours when folks aren't expecting a visit from the state. Mr.

Conners was found inside the home in the bedroom. The agent did her walk-through and saw more than one nights worth of clothes and belongings for Mr. Conners. While the worker was there, MiMi came in the house with groceries. After a few questions, she admitted she had been staying there for quite some time. I guess before, Ms. Williams could kind of predict when we were coming because it was always around the time for renewal of her license. I guess the timing got away from her and she wasn't prepared."

"So Mr. Conners was never a part of the licensing process?"

"According to my records, he was not."

"Okay," Fatima replied continuing to jot notes as Ms. Hicks spoke.

"Can you tell me the last kids in her home before it was shut down?"

"Let me double check my list, hold one second. I'm not going to put you on hold, just give me one minute."

The sound on the other end of the line became muffled as if Ms. Hicks put her hand over the speaking end of the phone. After a minute or so, the line was clear again, and Ms. Hicks spoke.

"Let's see, Gerald, Paul, Lacey and of course, Major was there."

"Four kids and three adults in a what, three-four bedroom double wide?"

Ms. Hicks didn't respond.

"So the four children were physically removed when?"

"Ms. Williams' license was revoked in July of 2015, and the three kids were taken out immediately. We didn't have places for them to go right away, though. You know it's hard to place teenagers, but we did get the three out in July."

"You keep saying three, but you named four youth," Detective Moore clarified.

"Oh, we took the foster children out. Major was still there."

"Why was he left?"

"Two reasons: one, he said he didn't want to leave and two, Ms. Williams had guardianship of Major, so he was not in our legal custody at the time. We had to petition the court to revoke guardianship, and once that was done, we were able to remove Major."

"And how long did that process take?"

"The total revocation process took a few months. I think it was after the first of the year before we got Major out of there. But I understand that even after all that legal stuff, Major ended up running from his placement and going back, more than once."

"I wonder what made him keep going back?" Detective Moore spoke her thought aloud.

"It's sad to say but where else was he going to go? I mean, with his history and everything? Not too many places would even consider taking Major. Besides, he'd been with Ms. Williams for years. That was probably the only family he knew, the only home he knew."

"Is it possible to get the record of placement on a few of these kids so we can try and track them down?"

"I will have to ask my supervisor about that and get back with you, detective."

"Well, you have my number. It did show up on your phone didn't it," Detective Moore asked.

"Yes, yes it did."

"Whether you get permission or not, please Ms. Hicks, give me a call as soon as possible and let me know. And if I'm not here, please leave a message, and I will call you back."

"Will do. Anything else, Detective Moore?"

"Not at the moment, but if I have more questions can I call you back?"

"Of course, and thanks for letting the Aiken County Department of Family and Children's Services serve you."

FIT

Detective Moore could tell that was a patented response, one Ms. Hicks probably said a hundred times a day. When the call ended, Moore reached out to one of the clerks in the office. They needed to interview as many of these kids as possible, as soon as possible. Locating them was going to be the problem.

"Clerk Styles," Detective Moore said with a bright smile.

"This cannot be good," Jack replied. He'd been a clerk in the Aiken office for several years and knew Detective Moore well.

"Aw come on Jack, don't do me like that," Detective Moore jested.

"Anytime you are bright eyed and smiling, that means work for me. Whatcha need, Moore?"

Moore handed Styles the list of names.

"I need to know where these kids are."

"Is this all you have to go on," Jack asked checking the scarcity of detail on the list.

"Yep."

Jack grumbled. "I need a dozen donuts, and not the cheap kind, and an iced coffee in the morning."

"I gotcha Jack! Have I ever not come through for you?"

Jack didn't respond. Fatima was confident Jack would handle it. He was good with information seeking.

Fatima stopped by the break room and grabbed a pop and some chips. That would be lunch for the day. Once back at her desk, Moore turned to her computer to run a few of the names through the criminal database. She was most interested in running Major Braggs.

Chapter Fifteen

Beth Ann arrived at the gym extra early. She was always excited when it was her time to work exclusively with Logan. Beth Ann knew she and Logan had a special relationship; one he didn't have with his other private clients. Beth Ann primped in the mirror, making sure she was ready for her one-on-one session with Logan. Beth Ann had on a new leotard, his favorite color, of course. She was clean-shaven in all the right places, lightly perfumed and her hair was freshly done.

Beth Ann would have looked silly with a full face of makeup. It was a workout session, after all, but she did make sure that her eyes popped with colors that matched her ensemble, mascara that extended her lashes, and her eyeliner was perfect. Pushing her size D cups up in her leotard creating a new line of cleavage, Beth Ann was ready to meet her trainer.

Logan had a particular plan for Beth Ann. She was very pliable, gullible even. Even though Logan liked to keep his own hands clean, he still had a murderous instinct. It had been awhile since someone took care of a problem for him. Beth Ann was poised to do her favorite trainer a favor. Logan did his own prep work, making sure he looked especially nice. It didn't take much for the likes of Beth to be smitten with him. Just like a bartender, his clients told him everything. He knew about Beth's sex life, or the lack thereof, from the long-term boyfriend who was more roommate than lover. She was starving for attention. Logan was prepared to give her just enough.

They met in the weight room of the gym. It was one of Logan's favorite spots for his personal clients. Enough people were working out to create the right amount of sexual tension; just enough women Beth Ann would try to make jealous, and the right number of men she could show off in front of. With his skill set and the need to instruct up close and personal, being in the weight room was the perfect setup. Logan could see Beth Ann coming through the door, wearing a broad smile; much too wide for her round face. That Cheshire grin she wore made her look fat. But Logan returned her smile as if he was really happy to see her.

"Are you ready, Beth Ann?"

"I was born ready, Logan."

He escorted his client over to the weight bench. Before he needed to tell her, Beth and was already lying down getting in position.

"Let's start with ten reps with the 35-pound weights," Logan instructed. "I will spot you."

"Okay, Logan," Beth Ann replied, still wearing that goofy grin. Logan lifted the barbell and lowered it over his client at chest level. Beth Ann pushed up from the bench, ensuring that Logan's hands grazed her breasts before he released the bar to her.

"Are you ready?"

Beth Ann lifted the barbell and Logan spotted her, counting as she went.

"And one. That's good Beth Ann, but make sure to keep your elbows relaxed and your arms straight. And three. Check your form. Make sure that you breathe, and five, six, seven, keep going eight. Two more Beth Ann, you got this, let's go. Nine and one more, ten."

Logan bent in his knees, demonstrating proper gym posture, and relieved Beth of the weights. After the first set, Beth repositioned herself on the pleather slab, making sure to extend her breasts which she thought would be attractive to Logan. Just before the next set started, Beth Ann scooted her head further up the bench which put her face almost at Logan's crotch level. Logan felt her encroachment and played on it, bending down seductively nearly grazing her with his manliness. Beth Ann moaned. Everyone in the weight room probably heard it.

Once they were done with the dead weights, Logan took Beth Ann over to another lifting station. This time, his client was positioned in front of a wall of mirrors which played into her desire to show off. It also gave Logan an opportunity to indirectly make eye contact with her.

After adjusting the weights on the bar, Logan helped Beth Ann put on a weight belt. He stood close behind her as he cinched in, pulling in her waist. Beth Ann watched him in the mirror, admiring his strong jaw, dreamy blue eyes, dark skin and strawberry blonde hair, cut close, accentuating the chisel of his face. Beth Ann pushed back against her trainer; feeling the strength of his pecs pressed against her back, the absence of a midsection touching her back, and the firmness of his manhood held loosely by his gym pants. Logan looked in the mirror and smiled. Beth Ann moistened.

"Do you remember what we worked on the last time we were together," Logan asked, still standing behind Beth, still allowing her the cheap thrill.

"I do," she oozed.

"Well, let's see if you can put it all together, okay?"

Beth Ann looked back over her shoulder. "Okay."

Bending down, without creating any space between them, Beth Ann reached for the barbell.

Logan stopped her with a firm hand to both sides of her waist.

"Forgetting something?"

Beth Ann stood up. "Oh, yeah, see Logan, you make it so hard to focus."

He laughed with her, accepting the compliment.

"What did you forget?"

"To bend my knees when approaching the dumbbell. Is that right?"

"You are such a good student," Logan complimented. "That is exactly right."

Beth took the instruction and did as her trainer asked, making sure to watch herself in the mirror to ensure good posture.

"Nice, Beth Ann, very nice," Logan encouraged.

He positioned himself immediately behind her and spotted her as she lifted the bar and stood back up.

"Now remember, every time you pull the curl bar to your chest, check your breathing and don't lock your legs. Got it?"

"Got it."

Beth Ann wanted to please him. Initially, when she came to the gym, it was to get back in shape for her man at home. The more he disappointed her, the less Beth Ann worked out for him. Her goal shifted. She wanted to please Logan. He encouraged her through each repetition, making sure to touch her intermittently as a reminder that he was there for her.

"I know you saw that little display the other day with Charlie," Logan began, setting the stage.

"I did," Beth Ann replied, still keeping her eyes on Logan through the mirror.

"I'm sorry you had to see that," he offered.

Beth Ann finished up her set and put the bar back on the cushioned mat. She turned to face Logan. There was minimal distance between the two.

"There's nothing for you to apologize for."

Logan took the opportunity to reach for a fresh towel. He extended the towel to Beth Ann, and when she grabbed it, he kept hold of it, assisting her as she dabbed the sweat from her face, neck, and chest. They maintained eye contact during the process.

"I appreciate you saying that, Beth," Logan began. "It's just that I don't want my clients to get the wrong impression."

"She was the one out of line, Logan," Beth asserted. "Anyone could see that you handle yourself professionally while she acted like a -," Beth stopped short.

Logan wielded an award winning smile.

"Like a what? Come on Beth Ann, you know you can tell me anything," Logan cooed.

Beth leaned in even closer, if that was possible, and positioned her lips just short of Logan's right ear.

"She acted like an old bitch," Beth Ann whispered.

When she pulled away from him, she looked to Logan for his approval.

He gave it to her with a wink.

"I just wish she wouldn't do that," Logan continued. "I mean, it could hurt my business here at the gym."

As he spoke, Logan turned Beth Ann by the waist back towards the mirror.

"Let's get ready for your next set."

She practically squealed with glee. Logan made her feel like a woman, a real woman; not the doormat her boyfriend treated her like.

Beth remembered her posture and bent her knees. When she returned to a standing position, Logan was there waiting for her.

He encouraged her through the reps, placing a hand under each elbow to assist with form.

"I just wish she would stop," Logan offered.

Beth Ann registered the gentle touch of his hand and his request subconsciously. Logan watched Beth Ann as her eyes tightened and her jaw clenched; indicators she got the message.

He repeated similar statements throughout the remainder of their session. When it was done, Logan offered one final suggestion.

"I wish all my clients were like you."

Beth Ann beamed. She knew she was his favorite, but Logan's last statement confirmed it. She would help her trainer out. Beth Ann didn't want his job to be compromised because some old woman couldn't keep her hands off him. Charlie had no couth. She was a threat. Beth Ann didn't like Logan to be threatened.

Making her way to the women's locker room, Beth Ann showered and changed into her street clothes. Before leaving, she signed up for her next private session with Logan. At $90 an hour, Logan wasn't an inexpensive indulgence, but he was worth every minute of it, according to Beth. While standing at the front desk, Beth casually checked Logan's time slots to see if Charlie snagged a private session. Not finding her there, Beth thumbed through a few classes and the relaxation room schedule. She knew Charlie was a fan of all things hot; hot tub, sauna, and of course, hot men like Logan. Beth took note of Charlie's sign up and walked out of the gym.

This was the worst part of Beth Ann's day. At the gym, she was free, carefree, with not a thought in the world other than her private time. But now it was time to go home. She knew her boyfriend would be waiting for her. He would grill her on where she had been, knowing she went to the gym at least four days a week. He would ask about the cost, and when she tried to avoid the subject, he would get loud and obnoxious. He already knew how much her private sessions were and he would harp on that until she was sick of hearing his voice. Yeah, this was the worst time of day for Beth Ann. Yet, Beth smiled as she got in her pickup truck. She did have something to look forward to, well actually a couple of things to be excited about.

She would see Logan again, within a few days. The other thing she was excited about? Resolving his little problem.

Grace was excited after speaking with Carmen. No matter the tough front Carmen put up, Grace was pretty confident she would be getting a phone call from her new girl any day now. When her children came home from school, Grace was excited to see them. She had their favorite dinner all prepared and paid attention as they recounted all their activities of the day. The whole family was seated at the dining room table when Drake got home. As he entered the kitchen, Grace got up from her chair and actually greeted him with a warm kiss to the cheek.

"How was your day, honey," she asked; relieving him of his attaché case and suit jacket.

Drake didn't know what to say, stammering when he responded. He couldn't remember the last time his wife acted like a real wife. Drake was so used to the snark, he looked bewildered.

"Come on, have a seat," Grace encouraged. "The children were just telling me about their day."

Drake did as Grace asked, looking zombified in the process. The kids were always excited to see their father and greeted him accordingly.

The family went through the entirety of the meal and evening activities like a typical suburban family. Drake waited until the children were put to bed and he and Grace were alone in their bedroom before addressing it.

"What was that all about?"

Grace busied herself in the adjoining bathroom. She had the door cracked so she could communicate with Drake. When Grace emerged, dressed in a sheer black negligee, Drake was flabbergasted. His mouth fell slightly open, and his eyes tracked her as she made her way to their bed.

"You were saying?"

His natural inclination was to forget about the conversation and follow his wife's sexualized lead. That was exactly what Grace wanted him to do, and Drake wasn't going for it this evening. He was sober, which helped, so he had greater clarity of thought.

Grace positioned herself right next to her husband, something else that hadn't happened in a while. Grace extended one hand, placing it on Drake's leg and the other on his bare chest. Looking up into Drake's eyes, Grace attempted to smolder. Drake couldn't believe that at one point he found any of her antics attractive.

When Grace leaned in to kiss him, Drake put up a cautionary hand. Grace was rebuffed.

"What was that all about, Grace?" Drake raised the question again, but Grace was not dissuaded in the least. Pushing passed his hand, Grace raised up on her knees and leaned her slight frame into her husband. He acquiesced and laid back on the bed.

"What, I can't be kind to my husband?"

"You can, if it's honest, Grace," Drake began, turning his head slightly as she leaned in for another kiss. Grace ended up kissing Drake on the cheek, but she made the most of it, tracing small kisses from his earlobe to his neck.

Drake caught a moan as it attempted to escape his throat. Grace had fallen in maintaining her wifely duty to sexually satisfy her husband. Drake couldn't remember the last time he actually had sex with someone other than himself. As Grace slid down, leaving trails of kisses as she went, Drake had a hard time keeping his manhood from responding.

"Grace, answer my question," he grimaced as his internal heat level started to rise. When she reached the top of Drake's pajama bottoms, Grace slid a bony hand down the front of them and began to massage Drake's member. This time, Drake couldn't muffle the groans. Drake sat up.

"Grace, this distraction isn't going to work. Answer my question."

This time when Drake spoke, there was no authority. He was more like whispers in the wind. Grace was unfettered in her quest, and eased the front of his bottoms down, freeing his manhood that was now standing at full attention. Drake wanted to fight it, he really did, but when she touched him, all the fight was zapped from him. Still, he insisted she answer his question.

Looking up from behind his member, Grace replied.

"I can't if my mouth is full."

With that, Grace descended on her husband, wrapping her taut mouth around his throbbing wood. Whatever objections Drake had they left the moment he felt her mouth on him. Drake watched her as she took him in. This was not his wife. She never incorporated oral sex in their marital bed, receiving and definitely not giving. Drake knew he couldn't trust it, but it felt so damn good. He laid back on the bed. What else could he do?

Grace was repulsed by what she was doing and fought against her natural predilection to choke. He didn't taste good, and she didn't like it.

However, Grace kept her real motivation in mind. She needed Drake to relax. When he relaxed, he wouldn't be so hard to deal with. Drake wouldn't protest when Carmen returned to their home. That was Grace's ultimate motivation, to soften her husband up. This was the way to do it.

"We found your daughter's car."

That was the gist of the conversation Tanner Sr. had with the Atlanta Police Department. Apparently, Tangela's car had been towed and was sitting in a tow yard. Because the bill had gone unpaid, the towing company was preparing to auction the vehicle off. The operator apparently passed the message along about his daughter being missing and with the license plate number, somebody did some checking, and they found Tangela's car. Tanner Sr. pressed for more detail. How long had the car been abandoned? Where was it towed from?

He got answers to his questions; answers that made him curious but not hopeful. There was a lot of time that passed since the car was towed. And still, there had been no contact from his daughter. The police promised they would follow up on the lead regarding the location of the car, and get back to him as soon as possible. Now all he and Tanner Jr. could do was wait.

Dorothy and Brett St. James, Madeline's parents, still hadn't heard very much from the Atlanta police as to what was going on with their daughter. The college she attended, sent an official letter that said absolutely nothing, in Mr. St. James' estimation. The university was covering its own ass and not very concerned about what happened with Madeline. The police had very little to go on. According to self-report, they interviewed Madeline's friends and classmates, but not much had come of it. Dorothy continued to be distraught. She wasn't sleeping well. Actually, she hadn't slept very much at all; just little cat naps here and there. Her inability to sleep impacted Brett. They were both on edge and their long-term marriage suffered for it.

People cope in different ways. The St. James' home was clean, spic and span and every day, Dorothy washed over places that were already spotless. The news was always on in the background, just in case there was breaking news about their own child. Brett took frequent trips to

Madeline's campus. He would park his car and watch the students making their way to class or converging on the square. Brett felt close to his daughter in those moments; visualizing her being one of the carefree students headed to class with a world of possibilities waiting for her.

Madeline's roommate, Nia, became a frequent guest in the St. James home. Everyone seemed to benefit from being together. They could speak openly about their concerns and fears, but it also gave the trio a chance to reminisce on the good times and build up hope. They never discussed Madeline in the past tense. It was always forward thinking. There would be tears, of course, with every gathering, but at least they were able to shed them together.

Chapter Sixteen

"We have got to make a move."

Chief Livingston didn't like operating this way. Breaching the perimeter of the facility had the potential of placing a lot of young kids at risk. Regardless of the pressure from the higher ups, Livingston wasn't willing to take that risk, not with such limited information. They had received phone calls and messages from some of the residents inside the facility, but nobody identified who the assailants were. And those who said they saw someone, couldn't tell if he was a resident, a staff person, or someone from the outside. The assailant operated with the benefit of poor lighting back where the resident's halls were, and no clear identification had come forward. Not up until this point.

"Chief, we've got another call," Dispatch Officer Cruz advised.

"Is it any good?"

"They are demanding to speak to the man in charge."

"Can we trace where the call is coming from?" Chief Livingston asked.

"It's coming from inside, boss."

Phillips and Daniels stood by. Chief Livingston accepted the phone and put the call on speaker for Michael and Chloe to hear.

"This is Chief Livingston. Who am I speaking with?"

"They said they would kill me if you all don't let them leave."

"Who is this?"

"Say just what I told you to say," Major threatened. The muzzle of his Glock lay against the temple of Mr. Franklin. He wheezed terribly.

Placing his hand over the phone, Mr. Franklin made a request.

"May I please have my inhaler... I can hardly breathe."

The break to his nose hadn't helped. Major looked at Mayven. He wouldn't make a very good hostage if he were already dead. Mayven cross the office and picked up the inhaler. She then walked over to Mr. Franklin.

"Are you going to be a good boy?"

Mayven waved the inhaler in front of Mr. Franklin as he fought for oxygen.

"Yes, yes I will."

"That's what I like to hear, obedience. Now, open your mouth."

Cornelius willingly complied, and Mayven compressed the activation button coating his throat with Albuterol. Cornelius breathed in to draw as much of the medication into his system as possible. With his eyes, he begged for another squirt and Mayven gave it to him. For the first time in hours, Cornelius breathed a lot easier.

Malcolm's previous cockiness had been taken down several notches. Malcolm heard the gunshot and the kids talking about somebody being dead. The same gun that shot one of his residents was now against the head of his co-worker. Although he liked Mr. Franklin, Malcolm was grateful they picked Cornelius. As long as he stayed quiet and didn't give them a reason, Malcolm hoped he would be alright. He hoped.

"Hello! Hello? Are you still there?" Chief Livingston called into the phone.

"Yes," Mr. Franklin replied.

"You said they. How many people are there with you?"

There was no response to the chief's question. "Tell whoever they are, we have the place surrounded. Tell them we are willing to negotiate as long as no one else gets hurt. Do you understand?"

Major and Mayven could hear the call on their end as well.

"Don't tell'em shit but what I told you," Major demanded.

"They said they would kill me if you don't let them leave."

Mayven disconnected the call.

"Dammit to hell!"

Chief Livingston was pissed.

"Get me a fuckin' hostage negotiator, now!"

Livingston damn near threw the phone at Cruz.

"Yes sir," Cruz replied. He walked away from the chief to make the necessary phone calls.

Dr. Daniels noticed something about the caller but decided to give the Chief a few seconds to calm down. Dr. Daniels watched as the Chief deescalated and then she waited for him to return to where she and Michael were standing.

"Chief," she began tentatively, just in case he wasn't all the way ready to hear what she had to say.

"Yes, doctor." Livingston sounded exacerbated, but Chloe pressed on. Although this wasn't her usual role in working with the police, that didn't stop Chloe from using her observational and assessment skills. If she was here, whether intended or not, she intended to be as helpful as possible.

"I noticed something about the caller," she offered.

Chief Livingston looked at her, encouraging Dr. Daniels to continue.

"His breathing. It was labored. He was struggling to breathe."

"You're right Chloe," Phillips added, not minding the informality in which he addressed her. "There was something odd about it."

"Well," Chief Livingston began, "That could mean one of a couple of things. Either he's injured, scared..."

"Or sick," Dr. Daniels added.

"Or sick," the chief repeated.

"Another thing," Chloe continued. "I would think, by the sound of the voice, this was an adult, a staff person. Most of the time, male staff manage boys in residential programs."

"Cruz!" The Chief bellowed.

Officer Cruz put his current call on hold and returned to where the Chief stood.

"Yes, sir?"

"Get me a list of the male staff on duty tonight."

"Yes, Chief."

"And Cruz, find out if anybody is sickly."

Andrea Braxton loved evenings like this. The temperature was perfect for a late evening stroll. A nightly walk was something she did routinely to relieve the stresses of the day. Most would caution a woman walking alone at night, but Andrea was not the least bit concerned. Not only did she live in a great, safe neighborhood, she had her insurance policies with her; Smith and Wesson, twin Bullmastiffs. At well over a hundred pounds each, Andrea comfortably walked through her Alpharetta Neighborhood. As she rounded the final corner before turning on her street, Smith and Wesson began to pull hard against their chain-link leashes.

"Boys! You know better than that," Andrea chided, trying to reign them in as best she could. Andrea was no match for the singular pull of one of her dogs let alone when the two pulled together. Smith and Wesson alerted to something, and once the mastiffs got the scent, nothing stood in their way. Andrea had no choice but to follow, and they dragged Andrea to a garage. Smith and Wesson pawed incessantly at the door that was partially opened. As Andrea got close to the garage, she smelled something that didn't smell quite right.

"Smith, Wesson! Come!"

The dogs were totally enthralled in the hunt. The marginal opening was no match for the intelligence of the dogs, and once Smith started to nudge the bottom of the door, Wesson joined in. The higher the door got, the more the malodorous stench wafted out. Andrea grew concerned. Not only were her dogs vandalizing some strangers' property, now they were breaking and entering. Both dogs were laying on their bellies fighting to get under the door. All the pulling in the world by Andrea did nothing to stop them. The leashes were snatched from her hands. Andrea was left standing in the driveway watching the situation unfold. She screamed for her boys, but they ignored her commands.

Wesson was the first to fully get under the door, and Smith quickly followed. With all of the noise and disturbance, lights started to come on in neighboring homes, and people began to emerge. The quiet of the neighborhood was disturbed. Andrea felt obligated to go in behind her dogs; to try and get them off this stranger's property. Running to the garage, Andrea lifted the door the remainder of the way. It was dark and difficult to see. There was no internal light coming from the house but the street light offered some illumination.

"Smith! Wesson! Come!"

Andrea walked up on her dogs. She pulled at Wesson's collar trying to get him back. He growled and then turned toward Andrea baring teeth. She was surprised by his response but then she got a glimpse of what drew both of their attention.

What she saw stopped her in her tracks.

"Oh my God, oh my God, oh my God," she cried as she backpedaled out of the garage, falling down and scrambling to get back up. Her screams brought neighbors into the driveway. One neighbor walked over helping to catch Andrea as she continued to stumble backward.

"What's going on?"

Andrea couldn't find words. Her eyes had to be deceiving her. They just had to be. The male neighbor asked again, and by this time, other neighbors encroached upon the driveway. When the concerned neighbor asked again, all Andrea could do was point a shaky finger at the garage. The neighbor followed her lead with trepidation. There were two massive dogs in the garage, and the sounds that emanated from and echoed within the small space was enough to frighten even the bravest soul. Andrea saw the neighbor advancing toward the garage, and she reached for him, fearful of what she thought she saw.

Trembling, Andrea's hands flew to her mouth, "No, don't!"

By this time another male neighbor joined the one walking toward the garage. The two men together got close to the entrance of the garage. Sensing a strange presence, one of the dogs raised their head and viciously barked. The men recoiled and rejoined Andrea midway the drive.

"Somebody get a flashlight or something," one of the concerned neighbors called back. Within minutes, the two men were equipped with flashlights. This way, they may not have to physically get as close to whatever drew the dogs in to get an idea of what was going on. The men checked in with each other. By this time, Andrea was completely freaking out. Again, they moved cautiously towards the entrance to the garage. Lights turned on and the travesty in the garage became crystal clear. The sight of dogs with bloody muzzles, baring razor sharp teeth, hovering over a body, temporarily froze both men where they stood. Eyes grew large; mouths fell open. One of the men dropped his flashlight. The other man reached out for the one, and they both fumbled back, much like Andrea, when all had not been revealed.

Once the two were back far enough for the dogs to lose interest in them, they both were shaken up.

Paul, the first concerned neighbor, was able to speak after a shocking moment.

"Somebody call 911!!!"

Chapter Seventeen

The response time for the Alpharetta police department was exceptional when compared to most police stations. Within minutes of the frantic call coming into the police station, officers were dispatched to 4821 Timberlake Drive in the affluent Timberlake Downs subdivision. The usually quiet neighborhood was lit with red and blue swirling lights and sirens blaring a warning that something was awry. When the call came into the police station, officers were alerted to the presence of vicious dogs on the premises. Animal control was dispatched with the police officers.

When patrol officers, Wallace King and Theo Coulter exited their squad car, they didn't approach casually. Both of the officers had flashlights and batons at the ready, to go to battle. Andrea was relieved to see the police, but she was also a dog owner. Smith and Wesson were the children she never had, and she didn't want anything bad to happen to them. From the officer's approach, she felt an additional unrest in her soul.

"What seems to be the situation," Officer King asked as the two made it to the center of the ever growing crowd where the reported witnesses were.

Paul Burton, one of the neighbors that came to Andrea's aid, was the first to speak.

"I think there's a body in that garage," Paul began, still pretty shook up.

"We could only get so close, you know, because of the dogs," Harold Blackstone, the second neighbor advised.

"Ma'am are those your dogs?" Officer Coulter turned to Andrea and asked.

"Yes, they're mine."

"And they wouldn't heel when called?"

"No, no they wouldn't."

As the officers spoke to the witnesses, the dog catching team arrived. Once their vehicle was parked, they joined the police officers. The catchers greeted the officers.

"This is the dog owner, Officer King advised.

Jim, one of the catchers, took over the conversation. His partner Clyde listened in.

"What kind of dogs, ma'am?"

"Bullmastiffs," Andrea answered.

"Their names?"

"Smith and Wesson," Andrea said, almost embarrassed, considering present company.

"But they're not vicious dogs, not in the least bit. I don't know what got into them, but they are good dogs."

"Okay, thank you, ma'am," Officer King advised.

"You all stand back," Coulter alerted.

Andrea, Harold, and Paul fell back and joined the rest of the crowd burgeoning on the edge of the driveway. The four first responders huddled. They came to a decision. The dogcatchers were armed with Tomahawk control poles. The police were armed with guns. Officers King and Coulter approached carefully with Jim and Clyde right behind them. They could hear the dogs. The smell of freshly spilled blood drifted from the garage. Both officers stopped midway the drive. Coulter abandoned his baton, holstered it and pulled out his standard issue Beretta. He took the safety off. Andrea saw the officer draw his weapon and her heart leaped. She moved in the direction of the garage and Paul grabbed her back.

In silence, the officers signaled to each other. Almost on cue, the garage was illuminated by their flashlights. Neither of the officers anticipated what they saw, nor did the dogcatchers. The unexpected light also drew the attention of Smith and Wesson.

Their natural inclination was to protect their kill. The humans were imposing on their claimed territory. Coulter leveled his Beretta. They would give the catchers an opportunity to try and control the dogs and remove them. But if that situation went south, the officers were prepared to use whatever level of force was necessary to gain control of the scene. Too much time had already been lost. There were no human sounds of pain or injury coming from the garage, but the officers had to operate as though there was someone in distress.

Jim and Clyde had their own way of communicating without speaking. Extending their control rods in front of them, the two began to move in sync toward the garage. King and Coulter took up the outer position, aligning themselves one with each dogcatcher. There was no conceivable way to get the dogs out of the garage without the catchers being able to contain them.

Wesson was the first to move; turning away from the body and towards those approaching. Standing firmly on all fours in attack position, Wesson growled at the intruders showing all his bloody k9s. Jim was the closest to the aggressive canine. Extending his trap rod in front of him, Jim made a slow but steady approach. Wesson zoned in on his movement and shifted his body in Jim's direction. When he did, Clyde moved up on the dog's blind side with his rod extended far in front of him. Wesson took a step in Jim's direction. Not backing down, Jim took another slight step forward, drawing the dog more in his direction so Clyde could complete the sneak attack. King and Coulter stood at the ready as well. Behind Wesson, Smith crouched low, shielding the body. Clyde's loop at the end of his rod hovered right in front of Wesson. When it looked like Wesson was turning towards Clyde, Jim took another step forward and extended his rod, distracting the growling dog. In an instant, Clyde slid his rod back and lassoed Wesson's neck.

As the trap cinched tighter, Wesson fought hard against it, barking and lunging at his perceived attackers. Seeing his twin being attacked, Smith leaped to his feet aiming straight for Clyde. Coulter saw the dog advancing on Clyde who was fighting to control the giant mastiff. Jim struggled to assist as the dog flailed too much for him to secure the trap line for added security. Smith charged the embattled dogcatcher. Andrea held her breath as the whole scene played out slowly in front of her. She moved again toward her babies, nearly breaking free from the neighbor holding her.

The shot from the Beretta rang out with a simultaneous yelp from Smith. Andrea screamed as she watched her dog falter and fall flat to the ground. King covered his partner as Jim and Clyde continued to try and wrestle Wesson into submission. When it looked as if Clyde was losing the battle, both officers leveled weapons at the thrashing dog.

"No! Please! No!"

Andrea screamed as onlookers watched the dramatic scene play out in front of them. Wesson fought hard, doing his best to get out of the chokehold the trap-line had on him. For a brief moment, Wesson landed on all fours, winded from fighting so hard. Jim was right there and quickly slid the trap collar around the dog's neck. Now both catchers had Wesson in their grasp and wouldn't let go. That only prompted the dog to fight more and fight he did. With renewed vigor, Wesson charged one and then the other. Jim and Clyde established a tug of war. When the dog went one way, they worked together to limit his advancement while at the same time trying to tire him out. Wesson was an alpha male and wouldn't submit.

The officers moved in closer, ready at any moment to intervene with deadly force. They could hear the woman screaming in the background to

FIT

spare her dog's life. But they had an obligation to human life.

"WEESSSOOONNN! Andrea screamed for her dog. "HEEEL WESSOONNN HEEEL!"

A dog knows it's master's voice. Something about her command resonated with Wesson, and he stopped fighting so viciously. Andrea saw her dog responding and continued to encourage him. She didn't know what Smith's fate was, but she had to fight to save her beloved pet.

"Please, Wesson! That's a good boy!" The man who had been holding her watched and saw what Andrea saw. Wesson was responding. Paul eased the tightness of his hold and Andrea moved toward her pet.

"That's right, that's mommy's good boy. Be a good Wesson for mommy," Andrea continued. The barking and growling stopped. Wesson settled down on all fours. Clyde and Jim didn't have to struggle as much. The police officers still held firm, but Wesson was in better control. Jim and Clyde waited a few more seconds before attempting to guide the dog out of the garage entrance.

"That's right. You're mommy's big boy, aren't you? That's a good Wesson."

Tears continued to fall from Andrea's eyes, but she would not relinquish. She had to do what she could to save him. Wesson was panting now. Fighting exhausted the heavy dog. Jim and Clyde took advantage of his weakened state and began directing him towards Andrea. That's where Wesson wanted to go. He wanted to be back with his owner. It was only then when the officers were convinced the catchers had complete control over the canine did they pull their fingers from the triggers of their weapons.

Andrea met Wesson as they led him away from the scene. Although his muzzle was bloody, he greeted his master enthusiastically. Jim and Clyde allowed the brief reunion before guiding the dog towards their vehicle. Andrea was glad to see that Wesson was safe. The catchers reassured her that they wouldn't leave the scene, but would put the dog in the back of the truck for his own safety. Once that was confirmed, and Andrea confirmed with Wesson that he would be back, she returned to the driveway area to see about Smith.

"Is my dog okay?" Andrea called out as she walked towards the officers.

"Is Smith okay?" Her persistence continued.

Officer King was the first to turn and address her.

"Ma'am we have to secure this crime scene. You are going to have to stay back."

"I just need to see if Smith is okay," Andrea continued. "He may need some help, and you're not letting me help him."

The tears were flowing again. While King was engaged with the dog owner, Coulter holstered his weapon, retrieved his flashlight from his work belt, and entered the garage. He hesitated, only taking a few steps inside so as to not further contaminate the crime scene. He could see the mutilated body of what appeared to be a woman on the ground. Her hair was muddied with blood. It would be easy to assume that no individual could survive the dual attack of the dogs, but he had a responsibility to check.

"Ma'am? Hello?"

There was no response. Coulter shone the flashlight on the concrete floor of the garage. He needed to get closer to confirm either life or death. Bloody paw prints streaked the garage's foundation. There was scarcely any clean area in which to walk. Coulter tiptoed over some prints and weaved his way as best he could to the body. Kneeling down, he got the first look at the damage. Coulter didn't want to turn the woman over, but he was able to access her wrist where he placed two fingers lightly to see if there was a pulse. He waited to see if there was any indicator. Coulter felt nothing. The officer lifted his flashlight to see if he could detect the rise and fall of the woman's chest. After a moment, he realized there was no movement. Standing to his feet, Coulter exited the garage as carefully as he entered. Officer King was still attempting to reason with the dog owner. When Officer King looked up and made eye contact with his partner, Coulter shook his head. The negative affirmation was enough for King to relinquish the denial to Andrea so she could see about Smith.

She ran the few feet to the fallen dog and fell to her knees next to him.

"Smith, baby, tell mommy you're okay, please be okay," Andrea encouraged as she checked her precious canine. His tawny coat was splattered with blood, and his muzzle was covered in blood. Andrea didn't know whether it was his or the poor woman on the inside of the garage. Andrea got as close as she could to Smith's face to see if there was any sign of life. Andrea laid across her dog's massive chest. If she could just feel his heartbeat, she would know Smith was okay.

But his heart didn't beat, and Smith didn't respond to her calls or her touch. Checking turned into collapse as Andrea realized the inevitability that Smith was indeed dead. She wailed for her precious canine, hugging his body, wishing he would come back to her. Officer Coulter stood by while Officer King reported into the station. They needed a crime unit and a coroner. Coulter empathized with Andrea. He had his own dog at home. Her wailing reached the ears of the bystanders, and a few of their hearts broke with hers. Never had they had anything like this play out in their neighborhood. Once King made the call to the station, he moved towards the crowd, encouraging them to remain at a distance as indeed this was a crime scene.

"Is it Leslie?" An older woman near the middle of the crowd called out to the officer. Hearing a name, Officer King made his way to her.

"Ma'am, do you know who lives here?"

"Why, yes I do," the little lady said in response to the officer's question. "That's Leslie's house, Leslie Viega. Is that her in the garage, officer?"

King neither confirmed nor denied but proceeded with a follow-up question.

"Do you know if anyone else lives in the house with Ms. Viega?"

Officer King took his pocket-sized notebook from his breast pocket and unclipped his ink pen. The street light was sufficient enough for him to see.

"No, there's no one else. She lives alone like me," the woman continued. "It's her, isn't it?" She pressed.

"And what's your name again," Officer King continued.

"Ruth, Ruth Clayborne," she answered.

"And where do you live, ma'am?"

Ms. Clayborne had her hand on her chest. This all had been a bit much for her. To think something like this happened in her neighborhood? She lived in Timberlake Downs now some 30 or more years. Nothing like this had ever happened before.

"I live across the street, and you have not answered my question, young man," Mrs. Clayborne asserted.

"I know, Ms. Clayborne, and I am not trying to be difficult. But if I can ask just a few more questions, it would really help us a lot." King felt chastised by his elder. But protocol required that he not respond prematurely in a situation like this.

"I understand, but this is very concerning, young man," Ruth continued.

"I understand, just one more question, please."

Ruth nodded her head in agreement.

"Can you describe Ms. Viega?"

"Oh, that's easy," Ruth confirmed. "Leslie is tall for a woman; I would say 5'9, 5'10, much taller than I am. But as they say, you shrink as you get older. Anyway, she is thin, always working out, but what do you young people call it, built – kinda busty, small waist and long legs. Let's see, she has medium length hair, kind of a fawn color, and green eyes."

As Ms. Clayborne described the woman, in his mind, King confirmed that's who was in the garage.

"I appreciate all your help, Ms. Clayborne. If you give me your exact address, I am going to give you my card just in case the investigating officers need to speak with you again."

Ruth complied and provided her address. As she accepted the card from the officer, he thanked her and started to walk away.

"Young man," Ruth called after him. "You still didn't tell me whether that was Leslie or not?"

Officer King paused, and the look on his face said what his mouth didn't. It only made sense that the person in Leslie's garage was indeed Leslie. But sometimes you hope that your inclination is wrong. This time, Ms. Clayborne's was not.

It didn't take long before an ambulance, and the coroner was on the scene. Additional officers also arrived and quartered off the crime scene with yellow caution tape. It was time for Andrea to move. Officer Coulter waited as long as he could, but now it was time for the scene to be processed.

Squatting down next to her, Officer Coulter spoke.

"I'm sorry ma'am, but I'm going to have to ask you to come with me."

"...you killed him..." Andrea's sobs were briefly halted as she addressed the officer without looking up.

Over the noise from all the activity, Coulter knew she said something, but wasn't sure what it was. He waited a beat and then addressed the grieving dog owner again.

"Ma'am, they have to process the scene, so we're going to have to move."

Coulter reached out his hand and touched Andrea on the shoulder. His touch was intended to be gentle and empathetic, but she shrugged him off harshly and repeated what she said the first time; this time loud enough for him to hear.

"You killed him!"

When Andrea turned to face the officer, her face was tear-stained, and her reddened eyes were narrow. Coulter understood her sentiment, but he had a job to do.

"Ma'am I'm going to have to ask you to vacate the scene." He spoke more sternly this time, and stood up, asserting his authority even more.

Andrea didn't want to fight with the officer. She was emotionally exhausted, but that didn't stop her from being angry at what transpired.

"You killed my dog, and now you want me to leave him? I can't leave him here with you people!"

Coulter got the attention of another officer who was approaching and waved him over.

"Ma'am I don't want to have to forcibly remove you, but you're not giving me a whole lot of choice. I know this is hard, but I'm going to have to ask you to stand up and leave with this officer."

"What are you going to do with Smith?"

"Ma'am, please," the officer replied sternly.

"What are you going to do with my dog?" Andrea was insistent.

"He will have to stay here for the moment, ma'am. As soon as we are able, your dog will be released back to you," Officer Coulter advised. "Now, please I need you to go with the officer."

Andrea complied, but not before giving Smith a hug and a kiss to his face.

"I'm so sorry…"

Peeling herself away from her pet, Andrea started to lift herself from the pavement. When one of the officers' reached out to assist, Andrea cursed them under her breath. She didn't want help from the people who murdered Smith. She made her way to the end of the driveway and under the caution tape, leaving her chaperone behind. Although pained, Andrea still had one of her boys. She made her way to the dogcatchers van and stayed with Wesson.

"What the hell happened here?" Detective Campbell asked as he walked up to one of the first responding officers.

"It's a fucking mess," Officer King reported. "Never seen anything like it."

Chief Celestine Granger, the first woman to rise to such a high rank in the Alpharetta Police Department, assigned the case to Detective Bryce Campbell. Campbell was a three-year veteran of her investigative team.

"Walk me through it man," Campbell replied. "Let's get some lights on this situation, please."

One of the crime scene technicians moved carefully to the back of the garage and with his flashlight, found a light switch. With the scene newly illuminated, the gravity of the matter was made clear. It was a blood bath.

Officer King recalled the first few moments upon arrival, not skipping any detail as Detective Campbell inspected the scene.

"One dog we had to put down, but the other is with the catchers."

FIT

Campbell was methodical. He didn't talk much when working a crime scene. For Campbell, there was so much more than the victim. Everything about a scene painted the picture of what actually happened. And he viewed it that way, inspecting every inch of the garage; from the spacing to the gym equipment, to the available entrances and exits. He looked for footprints and in the absence of them, what that may mean. The scene had been significantly contaminated by the presence of the animals. But were they the culprits? Or did something happen beforehand?

Campbell made his way over to the victim. Coroner Vickie Lucas was already there. She too was making observation and dictating her insights into a handheld recorder.

"Hey doc," Campbell greeted Lucas. "Give me the rundown."

"She's been dead less than 12 hours according to lividity and body temp. No real Rigor has set in, but that may have something to do with the dogs pulling and tearing at her flesh."

Candid was one word to describe Coroner Lucas. She didn't use a lot of flowery words, but Vickie was always solid.

"This is interesting," Lucas began. "I can't make a ruling as to cause of death just yet. The victim

237

could have had a heart attack or a stroke, or an accident of some kind. The dogs? They could be the culprits, but I won't be able to tell that until I can assess whether any of the bites were fatal."

"In other words, we don't know what happened here, is that right?"

"That's just about right."

Campbell lifted himself to a standing position. With one more peruse of the garage, he issued his first directive to the techs.

"Bag it and tag it all."

Chapter Eighteen

Even in solitary confinement, prisoners are allowed one hour of exercise. Anna looked forward to this time in her day. She got a chance to stretch her legs and see something other than the four blank walls in her cell. She was standing at the door when the guard came. Although Anna didn't have a watch to keep track of time, her internal clock tracked human interaction. That's what Anna missed the most, being able to interact with the people. Anna was sure they missed her too.

"Put your arms through the slot inmate," the guard instructed from outside the cell.

Anna didn't hesitate. The guard corralled her wrists into shackles.

"Step back."

Anna complied. The door to her temporary cage opened, and the guard ushered Anna into the hallway.

"No ankle chains," Anna asked.

"Plan on going anywhere?" The guard asked.

"Not today," Anna replied.

"Then we don't need them, do we?"

She was a new guard. Someone Anna hadn't had before. Anna was fine with no ankle holds. She hated the ankle chains the most. They made her walk funny. It was a short trip to the exercise yard. The guard called over the walkie-talkie to the guard station. There was a series of loud clanks and bangs as the mechanisms in the door gave way. The guard pushed the door opened and allowed Anna to walk out.

The exercise yard for solitary confinement was separate from everyone else. Anna would get no human interaction here other than with the guard if she chose to talk to her. At least it was another body present. The 'yard' was really more of an outdoors hallway, about the same length and width, with tall barbed wire fencing on three sides. The wall of the jail made up the fourth wall. The best part about it for Anna was the ability to look up. There was sky there with no chains and no fences and nothing that made her feel like a trapped animal. The sky was vast and expansive and full of possibilities.

In the cell, Anna was haunted by her own thoughts. Most recently, those thoughts were of her sister, Angel. Surprisingly, Anna had moments of real sadness when it came to her sister.

"The infamous Anna Black."

The guard addressing her drew Anna away from her sky gazing.

"You do know you're famous, right?" Officer Lenore Williamson asked as she leaned against the only solid wall in the exercise space. Anna didn't respond.

"I watch you, every night on the news, they talk about the infamous Anna; serial killer, Angel of Death... ewwwww..."

Anna returned her gaze upwards.

"Why'd you do it?" Williamson pressed, leaving the wall and walking in Anna's direction. The guard's movement drew Anna's attention.

"I don't know what you mean," Anna replied.

"Come on Anna," Williamson began. "Ain't nobody out here but me and you. You can tell me. I ain't gone tell nobody."

"There's nothing to tell, officer."

"I understand," Williamson continued. "It's smart not to say anything to incriminate yourself. I get it, I mean, you don't know me, whether I'll snitch or whatever."

Williamson walked as she talked, circling Anna.

"Did you know you have fans, Anna?"

"What do you mean?" Anna was actually intrigued.

"Of course, they wouldn't tell you," Williamson scoffed. "You have a ton of fans, girl! The jail gets boatloads of mail every day addressed to Anna Black, Angel of Mercy."

"Really? People are sending me letters?"

"Oh yeah, lots of them. But that's not all," Williamson continued. "It's people outside of here right now with signs saying, 'Free Anna', 'Let our Angel Go'," Williamson added. "Crazy right?"

"I have fans?"

"Yep, you sure do," Williamson confirmed.

"That is crazy."

Anna continued a slow traipse around the yard. A slight smile creased her face as she considered what the guard said. There were people in the world who understood her. That made Anna feel good. She wasn't alone. People truly understood and cared.

"Hey officer," Anna asked, turning to face Williamson. "Do you think they'll let me see those letters?"

"I don't know, Anna," Williamson replied. "I'm surprised your lawyer didn't tell you about them."

"I'm not," Anna rebuffed. "He was a worthless piece of court-appointed shit."

Williamson laughed with the inmate. She knew all too well about the public defender's office. The wheels in Anna's mind started to spin.

"He didn't tell me, but he could have," she began, as much to herself as to the guard. "Seeing as I am my own attorney now, maybe I can get my hands on those letters. I mean, they're addressed to me, right?"

"Officer, can you let your boss know my attorney has a legal request?"

Williamson smiled. Anna was not nearly as bad or as scary as people made her out to be. The other guards talked so bad about her like Anna Black was the devil reincarnate. But Williamson didn't get that impression at all.

"I sure can, Ms. Black."

It was nearing the end of Anna's time in the yard. She'd grown quiet, contemplating what Williamson said. To know she had fans and people that really cared about her made Anna smile. But that smile soon faded as thoughts of Angel crept back in.

"Officer Williamson?"

"Yes, wassup, inmate?"

"Just one more thing," Anna replied, leaning against the fencing. Williamson stood in the middle of the narrow runway.

"My baby sister passed away the other day."

Sorry to hear that," Williamson offered.

"Thanks," Anna somberly replied. "Problem is, nobody has said anything about her funeral. Will I get to see her? Will they let me attend?"

"Now that I don't know about, Anna," Williamson maintained.

"I mean she's my kid sister," Anna whined. "I would at least like a chance to say goodbye, you know?"

"I understand," Williamson offered. "But they probably won't let you. I know of other inmates who've lost family members, even their children, and they weren't allowed to go to the funeral."

Anna's head dropped. That wasn't promising news. Williamson noticed how sad the inmate looked.

"Tell you what," Williamson began. "When I check with my supervisor about the letters, I'll ask about the funeral too, okay?"

Anna lifted her head. What the guard offered wasn't expected, but Anna definitely appreciated it.

"Okay."

Cruz had done an admirable job gathering the information Chief Livingston requested. Fortunately, Devereux kept fairly good records of staff on duty, and with a little push, provided Cruz with personal information about the dozen or so staff that were working that night back in the cottages. The list of names included six men. That's the list Cruz provided to the chief. Livingston eagerly reviewed it, looking for ailments or physical predicaments that could potentially narrow down the list even more.

"Phillips, Daniels, take a look at this," Chief Livingston said.

They both leaned in, looking closely at the details listed by each of the male staff persons.

"What about this one," Phillips said, pointing to a name on the list."

Livingston and Daniels zoned in on Phillips discovery.

"Older, asthmatic, that could be it," Dr. Daniels offered.

"Cruz, does it say what cottage Cornelius Franklin is assigned to?"

Cruz looked over his notes from various conversations with Devereux staff.

"Yes sir, it does," Cruz replied. "He's assigned to Brigadoon."

"We may be on to something here," Chief Livingston replied. For the first time since the call came in, Livingston felt like they were indeed moving in the right direction.

"Cruz, I need to know every kid in Brigadoon and who else is on staff with him."

"You got it, Chief."

"Now that you feel better Mr. Franklin, you can make another call," Major stated.

"Why are you doing this, son," Mr. Franklin asked, trying to remain as still as possible. Major still had the gun to his temple, and Mr. Franklin didn't trust Major's trigger finger.

"Don't start that shit with me, Frank," Major said, waving the gun in the air and then replacing it; pressing the muzzle a tad bit harder against Mr. Franklin's skull.

"Major, I promise, I am not trying to start anything," Mr. Franklin reasoned. "I'm just trying to understand, son."

"I'm not your motherfuckin son!" Major exploded and in doing so, forcibly pushed Mr. Franklin's head with the muzzle of the Glock. "That's the fuckin problem right there!" Major released the pressure against Mr. Franklin's face and momentarily walked away. Mayven could see him escalating. She recognized the signs all too well. Mr. Franklin was barking up on his own demise.

"You are the reason I came back to this bitch, you motherfucker, you..." Major paced for a second and then leaned against the office wall. He wore a grimace, and his brow was low.

Mr. Franklin looked confused by the young man's comments but thought better of saying anything. He didn't need to. Major gave him insight before, but now he intended to break it all the way down for Mr. Franklin.

"It was you, always comparing us to your perfect kids... you probably thought that shit was encouraging somebody, but it wasn't... You found a way to make kids who already didn't feel, feel even worse, cause now, we wasn't measuring up to your fuckin standard. That ain't what you here for man! That ain't the kind of bullshit you tell kids who struggling to find they way. That shit you was talking then and probably still talking was some hurtful shit, for real. And I intend to make you pay for every single word of that bullshit... for real tho... every m'fuckin' word."

Whatever desire Mr. Franklin had to try and reason, left him.

"So them perfect punk ass sons of yours, Frankie? I hope you told them bastards you love'em cause I intend to orphan they asses today..."

"Then let me go then," Malcolm chirped up. "I didn't know you before, and I ain't done nothin' to you so y'all should really just leave me out of this."

"Now, see, we really had stopped fuckin' with you. And quiet as it's kept, we planned on leaving you right here," Mayven began. "But you the kind of nigga that run your mouth a lil too much. You don't know when to shut the fuck up and just ride shit out."

Mayven tossed Mr. Franklin's inhaler to the floor and reached for her blade.

"Hey bae, you think we got room for two in the back of the ride?"

"Let me think about that shit for a second... hell motherfuckin naw. That'll be a tight ass squeeze," Major chimed in.

"Yeah, you right, boo. That would be a tight ass squeeze."

Malcolm formed his lips to protest, but it was too late. Mayven turned the blade, took a step and sliced his throat. Blood poured from the clean slice across Malcolm's neck. His head flopped like a ragged doll. He didn't say shit else.

Mr. Franklin gasped. This was all such a nightmare. Without prompting, he started to wheeze.

"Now about that phone call..."

When the phone rang this time, Chief Livingston was more prepared. He had a pretty good idea of who he was talking to, at least. He put the call on speaker and Phillips and Daniels listened in.

"This is Chief Livingston."

"They told me to tell you to clear the gate and move your men back. If they see any cops, they will kill me."

"Mr. Franklin, Mr. Cornelius Franklin?" Cornelius didn't respond. His heart cried out to, but the looks he received from his captors told him he better not.

Mayven looked at Major. The police knew exactly where they were.

Dr. Daniels clued in on the call.

"Stick to the script, motherfucka," Major threatened.

"Do you understand they will kill me if you try to stop them or follow them?"

"Yes, tell them we understand," Chief Livingston said.

"We will be leaving in a few minutes. Please," Mr. Franklin begged. "I don't want to die! Keep your promise, okay? I don't want to die!"

The phone call ended abruptly. Chief Livingston went into action. Phillips, you and the doc get in your vehicle. I want you off the premises but close enough to the interstate to follow at a safe distance. Cruz radio the helicopter, tell them to fall back. No lights, none!"

Chief Livingston got on the police intercom. "All officers, fall back. Give me a one-mile radius all the way around the facility. Officers on foot, remain out of sight. Keep a visual but do not let the suspects see you. Is that clear?"

Phillips and Dr. Daniels didn't hesitate to move when the captain said move. They weaved their way through the plethora of police officers and the quartered off media personnel. Once they were back in the vehicle, Michael turned the red and blue flashers on, only enough to get better access to the place where he would post up. It would be a waiting game after that.

"This is kind of scary."

"What do you mean," Michael turned in the drivers' seat to face her.

"This whole hostage situation," Chloe answered, turning slightly to face him.

"First time?"

"Of course," she chuckled. "I usually show up after it's all over."

"Ha," Michael chuckled. "I never really thought about it like that. I guess this would be pretty scary then."

"Yeah, pretty damn scary."

Dr. Daniels phone chirped. Chloe retrieved it from her pocket. She was already prepared to roll her eyes in the event it was Nigel. Chloe was relieved to find it was Addison. She read the message that was surprisingly all in capital letters.

CALL ME, PLEASE!

Addison was not prone to having a dramatic flair. Chloe hit the speed dial button, and her assistant answered on the first ring.

"Are you okay?"

Addison sounded panic-stricken.

"I have been watching the news and seeing all the armed police officers, and the helicopters, and they said a kid was dead and…"

"I'm fine, Addison, I'm fine," Dr. Daniels confirmed.

"Whew, okay… I'm sorry, but I hadn't heard from you, and all this stuff was happening, and I knew you were out there…"

"I should apologize to you for not checking in. I'm sorry about that," Dr. Daniels offered.

Addison took a deep breath.

"Just as long as you're okay, I mean really okay."

"Yes, I'm with Detective Phillips, and I'm fine," Dr. Daniels replied trying her best to be reassuring.

"Okay, that's good to know because if anything were to happen to you Dr. Daniels I don't know what I would do."

Addison's voice cracked as if she was on the verge of tears. It was endearing, and Chloe realized how remiss she had been for not checking in sooner.

"I promise I will check in with you in a little while."

Dr. Daniels disconnected the call.

"She was worried about you, huh?"

"Yeah, and I feel so bad," Chloe replied. "It never crossed my mind that she would worry like that."

"Well, it made me feel good to hear you say you were safe with me," Michael admitted.

"Well Detective Phillips," Chloe teased. "Am I not safe with you?"

"Chloe, I would lay down my life for you."

His response was weighty and unexpected, but Chloe kept it light.

"Isn't that the policeman's duty to all citizens?"

"True, it is," Michael agreed. "But I would willingly sacrifice for you."

She felt her cheeks warm, and an inescapable smile touched her lips. Chloe turned her face away from Michael, not wanting him to see her blushing. He caught her gently by the chin and redirected her back to him. Their eyes met again in that moment. The energy between the two was palatable, and Michael leaned in. When Dr. Daniels did nothing to resist, he kissed her; gently at first, and when there was willingness found in her lips, Michael kissed her passionately. Chloe gave in. The shock of Michael being forward soon wore off as she allowed her guard to slowly fall, and she kissed him back. Their heated entanglement was long overdue, and Michael relayed that message to Chloe with his impassioned kiss.

Beth Ann was very excited about the day's prospects. Just like clockwork, Charlie was at the gym, flaunting around in a dated velveteen jogging suit and gold Lemay sneakers; impractical for really working out, and bouffant hair that reached the ceiling. Charlie was loud and obnoxious. Beth

Ann intended to rectify that situation. Today was different for Beth in the sense that she wasn't preoccupied with Logan. She would see him, in due time, and when she did, Beth would have great news to report.

So she stalked Charlie as she pretended to work out and flirted with anything with a penis.

"...so predictable..." Beth Ann thought to herself as she operated the elliptical machine not far from where Charlie was. After about an hour, Charlie retired to the women's locker room where she changed into a two-piece floral bathing suit that did nothing for her shape. Beth Ann watched her and waited.

Beth Ann waited until Charlie was in the sauna, comfortable and alone. With one turn of the dial, the heat index in the enclosed room went from 90 degrees centigrade to 160. With the Fahrenheit temperature reaching nearly 320 degrees, it wouldn't be long before there was no oxygen for the fair Charlie to inhale and no way to leave with a chair propped against the knob. She would sweat, and she would burn, and she would die...

"You did good, old man," Major snarled, hitting Mr. Franklin squarely in the back. "Just keep playing along, and I might let yo' pompous ass live."

"We gotta move, bae," Mayven suggested; wiping her knife off on Malcolm's pants leg. She moved over to where Mr. Franklin was still tethered to the chair and sliced through the duct tape, freeing him on one side and then the other. Mr. Franklin relaxed a bit in the chair as the tightness of the tape had restricted not only his movement but his breathing. Major snatched Cornelius up from the chair and put the Glock in the center of his back.

"Im'ma tell you like I told them kids. Scream, I'll kill you. Do anything to draw attention to this situation, I will kill you. Got it?"

Mr. Franklin nodded his head. "But can I please have my inhaler?"

Mayven scooped the inhaler off the floor and shoved it in her back pocket. She was sure Mr. Franklin would never have another opportunity to use it, though.

They were taking a hell of a risk in trying to get from the cottage to the car, but if they allowed themselves to be trapped on the premises, Major and Mayven knew they couldn't win. They were outmanned and outgunned.

"Kiss for luck," Mayven asked as they made their way to the back of the cottage. Leaving out the front door could be walking into a trap. The police were not known for their honor, so the coverage the cottages provided would help them get to the car.

"Im'ma kiss you 'cause I love you, fuck luck," Major answered, leaning over, deeply kissing Mayven. As they separated, the two shared a moment.

"Love you, man."

"Love you, too."

Mayven was the first to the back door. With the kill bag in one hand and her blade at the ready, Mayven moved slowly. She looked in both directions before waving to Major to bring the hostage out. Before he reached the threshold, Mayven threw up her hand indicating stop. She heard something. There was something or somebody moving behind the cottage next to Brigadoon. Mayven reached for her blade and held it firmly in front of her. Major started to speak, and Mayven held up her hand again.

"Psst..."

Somebody was trying to get her attention.

"May, it's me Pinky."

"The fuck?" Mayven breathed a sigh of relief and breathed even easier when Pinky emerged from the shadows with her hands up.

"Pinky, you almost got yo ass killed fuckin' around out here," Mayven scolded. It was only after hearing who Mayven addressed, did Major relax a bit.

Pinky fully emerged and met Mayven at the back door.

"What the fuck are you doing out here, Pinky?"

"We been watching everything going down on the TV, and I figured you might need some help or something."

"Good looking out Pinky, but this some dangerous shit right here, fam. I can't get you caught up in this for real."

"May, you know I love you like a sister. Ain't nothin' I wouldn't do for you. So you say the word and I'll help you any way I can."

"I appreciate that girl, but I can't. I wouldn't be able to live with myself if something happened to you, Pink, but you know I appreciate you though."

"I hear you."

Mayven could hear the disappointment in Pinky's voice.

"Seriously, Pink, I appreciate you girl," Mayven said opening up her arms. Pinky walked in willingly hugging May back.

"...take me with you..." Pinky whispered in May's ear.

Mayven was surprised and pulled back and looked to see if Pinky was serious. She quickly saw that Pinky was.

"Damn, Pink, I wish I could," Mayven started.

"I promise May, I won't be no problem I can help y'all. Hell, you know how I get done. You got his six, and I got yours, shoot'em up bang bang and shit."

"This ain't no play, play stuff, Pink and I can't be responsible for nothing happening to you like that."

"What do I have to lose, May? I'm already in hell. What the fuck I got to lose, for real?"

Mayven didn't have an answer for that. She knew all too well the pain Pinky felt. But her allegiance was to Major. Taking on somebody else like that, putting another person in harms' way, Mayven couldn't do it. And Pinky saw the answer before Mayven ever spoke.

"It's cool, naw for real, it's cool." Pinky's disappointment was so clear on her face it nearly broke Mayven's heart. Because of the scarce light, Mayven didn't see Pinky's eyes swell with tears, nor the one's that found their way down her saddened face. Pinky didn't let the tears remain too long as she swiped at them viciously before speaking again.

"No problem May, I still got yo back. Whatchu need me to do?"

Mayven checked in with Major. He heard Pinky's offer and saw Mayven's concern. He gave her the nod signaling his approval for Pinky's involvement. Mayven turned back to Pinky.

"We need to get to the parking lot behind the cafeteria. Be our lookout."

"Gotcha."

Pinky was heartbroken, but still, she wanted to help her friend. Anybody who could stick it to the man, and fuck with the establishment like May did, yeah, Pinky was down for it. Pinky looked up to Mayven. She was one of the only girls that ran from Devereux and didn't get caught. Mayven came back on her own terms. That was some shit to be proud of. Pinky looked back to Mayven to see if they were ready to move out. When Mayven gave her the nod, Pinky crouched low and started to move around the back of Brigadoon. Major fell in line with Mr. Franklin in tow. They all rounded the back of the building. Pinky stopped short the first time she saw one of the residents posted up in front of the window looking scared for his life. Mr. Franklin also hesitated as he passed and by the third window, he paused, seeing how scared the resident actually was. It looked like the boy wanted to say something to him but with Major quickly coming into view, hesitated. Whatever words the kid wanted to say, they stopped short at the sight of Major and his gun.

When Pinky reached the edge of the cabin, she stopped altogether. She didn't want to put the people who were counting on her at risk, so she took an extra moment to stop, look around, listen and make sure the coast was clear. In the other cabins, not directly affected by Major and Mayven's presence, staff instructed the residents to stay inside. They were tuned into the news, and the director contacted every cabin and gave clear instructions. That's the only reason the area was free of spectators and bystanders. It was too dangerous for anybody to be out of the cabin with suspects on the loose. Only when Pinky was completely satisfied did she move out, staying low, and making sure not to get too far ahead of her charges that she lost contact with them. Everybody stayed close.

Mr. Franklin moved a lot slower than the rest of the group. He looked over in the pasture in front of the cabin and saw the body still there, untouched. It was real. It was true. They killed Maurice. Mr. Franklin fully expected, even hoped that there would be people outside, somebody that could see what was going on. He didn't get the benefit of the phone call from the director saying otherwise.

Mr. Franklin paused a little too long, but Major made sure his feet kept moving until they reached the protection of the next building. Everybody's eyes were peeled just in case the police tried to be slick.

"Keep it moving, old man," Major threatened as they faced the largest clearing of their escapade. He kept the Glock jammed into the back of Mr. Franklin as the group moved forward. The car was just a few feet ahead. The group moved from grass to pavement, and in doing so, Cornelius' feet got tangled up, and he stumbled and fell.

"Son of a bitch!" Major hissed. "Get yo ass up!"

Mr. Franklin was doing the best he could, but all the fast moving made it even harder for him to breathe. He had been injured in the cabin and now with this fall, busted his knee cap open. He only knew that because of the stabbing pain he felt. Cornelius knew neither of these people cared so he took his pain and did his best to keep up. He was a man of faith. Mr. Franklin was convinced God would see him through this situation. He remembered one of his fondest quotes. "God gives his hardest challenges to his toughest soldiers."

Cornelius would hold on to that to get him through.

Once the group was at the car, Major used his free hand to dig in his pocket and get the key fob.

"We need to tie his hands," Mayven suggested. Major agreed. She was always thinking. Mayven was always one step ahead. Dropping the kill bag to the pavement, Mayven fished out another roll of duct tape that was shoved near the bottom of the bag. Pinky was all too happy to assist in binding Mr. Cornelius' hands in front of him. Pinky tore the end of the tape off with her teeth and deposited the remainder back in the bag. Hitting the button to activate the locks, Major maneuvered Mr. Franklin around the girls and ushered him into the back seat. Major locked Cornelius down with the seatbelt. Then and only then did he temporarily shove his gun in the back of his jeans and grab up the bag to put in the trunk.

"Well, I guess that's it," Pinky started, still looking around to make sure the coast was clear.

"Thanks, Pink, for real."

"Hey, what are friends for," Pinky asked, reaching out to May and pulling her into a big bear hug.

"Be safe," Mayven said as she parted ways with her friend.

"You, too," Pinky answered. "I ain't gone say see you later, just go kick some ass."

"You already know," Mayven called back.

Mayven made her way to the passenger side of the car. Once she was inside, Mayven put her blade on the floorboard in front of her. She was much more comfortable having her weapon within close reach, just in case. Major finished up in the back and climbed in the passenger seat. He put the Glock on his leg before firing up the car.

"No lights..."

Major fired up the ignition.

"Stay low, boo," he instructed Mayven.

Putting the car in reverse, Major backed the car out of the parking space. It had been quiet so far, no evidence of police on the premises. But Major was nobody's fool. He knew the cops had something planned for them and he was ready for whatever. Once the car was in drive, Major navigated the speed bumps until they got close to the entrance of the property.

"If it's going down May, it's going down right here," Major warned.

Mayven picked up the Glock. She was no stranger to weapons. It was locked and cocked within an instant.

"I got you."

"You can still stop this, right now," Mr. Franklin chimed in, breaking the confirmatory moment between the two.

Mayven was first to move. Getting up on her knees and leaning to the back, Mayven lifted the gun.

"Open your mouth," she ordered. When Mr. Franklin was slow to respond, she jammed the muzzle of the Glock in his lips and forced them open.

"Say one more thing and you won't have to worry about Major," she threatened. "You in the car now, bitch. They don't know if you alive or dead. You still a fuckin' hostage so keep yo goddamn mouth shut."

She watched as his eyes registered that she meant business. Snatching the gun from his mouth, Mayven turned around and sat back down in the passenger seat like nothing happened.

"Like I said, ready when you are, boo."

It was time. Major crept the car forward. They both knew enough to know that the gate would open from the inside once the street and call box detectors noted the presence of a vehicle. They would have to wait until the twelve-foot barbed wire gate crawled back on its track before the car could pass.

"Wait!" Mayven said, placing her hand across Majors' chest to make sure he understood. "We need to change his position.

"That's too fuckin dangerous, May. We almost at the gate," Major warned.

"Bae, if they don't see him, they ain't gone believe we got' em. He needs to be in the front seat until we clear these fools."

What she said made a lot of damn sense. Major didn't argue. Instead, he threw the car in park, jumped out of the driver seat and opened the back door. He quickly unbuckled Mr. Franklin and dragged him out of the car. At the same time, Mayven got out of the front passenger seat and made her way around to the drivers' side. When Mr. Franklin was secure in the front, Major met Mayven on the passenger side of the car. She gave the Glock to Major and climbed in the drivers' seat and Major positioned himself in the back. Mayven thought it better if she was driving. They wouldn't shoot a girl, would they?

"Now we ready."

Putting the car in drive, Mayven eased the car to the call box. She looked around. Major told them through Mr. Franklin to clear the front of the property. Mayven looked hard trying to see through the shadowy darkness but she didn't detect anything. Maybe they did what they were supposed to do? Mayven didn't know but she didn't trust that shit. Major was positioned with the Glock to Mr. Franklin's temple, visible from all sides of the car. If the police rolled up on them, they would have to take out the hostage, too.

It felt like the gate was taking forever to respond.

"Come on, motherfucka, come on," Mayven chanted as they waited for the first indicator that it would move. If the police had been smart, this hesitation would have been the perfect opportunity to collapse on the trio, but all was quiet.

And then it happened. There was a whine and then a loud click and the gate began to eek back.

"Come on, baby, open yo ass up," Mayven encouraged. Adrenaline flowed freely through her veins. She knew this could very well be the end for them, but Mayven promised herself she would never live with regret. Nothing she had done over the past few days did she feel the least bit of guilt or sadness about. Everybody they offed deserved what they got, maybe more. If this was her time to go, she couldn't think of anyone better to leave this world with than with Major. He was the foundation she was able to stand on. He never wavered and never made her question whether or not love was possible. Major loved her. That she knew for sure.

When the gate was back far enough for the car to pass through, Mayven looked in the rearview mirror. He was there, right there with her and she felt her soul connection. She was his ride or die. They had a blood pact they were both willing to honor to the bitter end.

Mayven eased the car to the gate and paused. She checked in again, looking for the tale-tell signs of the police. None were to be found. Easing the car forward, Mayven paused again and then crossed the raised edge indicating they breached the gate. Major sat up further in his seat, ensuring his gun was at the ready. The only thing Mr. Franklin could do was hope and pray.

They passed the security guard hut. No police. Mayven eased the car around the first corner. Still, no police. She refused to breathe any sigh of relief until she and her man were out of this predicament. A long horn blared out and everybody in the car jumped. It was the train, alerting that it was moving down the track. The presence of a train was a good and bad thing. It would stop the police from approaching on Mayven's left but it also limited how they could get to the interstate. Mayven paused again since everything seemed to be clear until the train reached where the car was and then she rode along with the train using it as a moving shield.

They turned the corner away from the flashing lights of the railroad crossing and still there was no sign of police presence.

Chapter Nineteen

The blaring train horn put the police on edge as well. Just like for those trying to escape, the train had its pros and cons. Chief Livingston wasn't close enough to see the train, but he knew the layout of the land. Unless the assailants were foolish enough to wait for the train to pass, they only had one way out. They would have to travel down Stanley Road to Stilesboro Road NW and then to Ernest W. Barrett Parkway. That was the fastest route to Interstate 285 in either direction. Livingston had police posted up on New Salem, the next side street and at Mt. Paran Christian School that sat at the intersection of Stilesboro and Ernest Barrett. The police had cover there, and unless the assailants were looking for them, they wouldn't be seen. Livingston alerted over the intercom to his officers to stand at the ready. Each post had a point person for the chief to communicate with. He expected his point people to check in if and when they saw the assailants. Phillips was posted up the closest to the highway.

On top of everything else, the media continued to be an issue. When the police moved, they moved. Among the other things the chief had Officer Cruz doing was contacting the heads of the local television stations to get their correspondents out of the way. First Amendment rights and freedom of the press were being tossed around all over the place. Cruz had the authority to threaten criminal prosecution to any correspondent who knowingly or unknowingly impeded the successful apprehension of these suspects. Cruz didn't know how effective the threat would be, but he made it with vigor. All the police could do now was wait for the suspects to show themselves.

Mayven took the corner and proceeded cautiously down the residential street. Window drapes were pulled back, but the street was vacant. Everybody in the area knew what was going on, but they still didn't know who was doing it. The area was under siege, and nobody was willing to take a chance on a stray bullet finding them. As the car neared a minor intersection, Mayven eased the car forward to get a better look.

"Easy May," Major encouraged. She didn't verbally respond, only nodded her head acknowledging that she heard him. Out of her periphery, Mayven spotted a dark car facing the intersection just shy of the stop sign.

"There you are," she cooed. Mayven marked the police car trying to play incognito. Major posted up, getting a look at the car for himself. He made sure anybody looking could see the gun pressing the temple of their hostage. Mr. Franklin's eyes grew large. The police hadn't done what they promised they would do. They lied, and it could cost him his life. But no lights ignited. No sirens blared, and the car didn't move. Mayven eased their vehicle right on by.

Inside the squad car, a call went out to the chief that the culprits were spotted. The officer also confirmed the hostage was inside the vehicle. He and his partner both could see it from their vantage point. Chief Livingston took note. The intercom system allowed the other officers to hear what was going on. Chief Livingston alerted the officers at the school to be ready.

"How are the police going to apprehend the suspects," Chloe asked shortly after their heated kiss.

"Right back to business, huh?" Michael said laughingly.

"Well, we are kind of on a stakeout, Detective Phillips."

"You're right, Dr. Daniels," he agreed, moving back over on his side of the truck and straightening out his clothes.

"The kiss was nice," Chloe offered as a consolation prize, but she raised the question again.

"Best case scenario? Spike strips on the interstate after it's cleared. Car disabled, police surround, negotiate for the hostage and take the assailants in."

"That's the best possible scenario," Chloe asked. "That doesn't sound good at all."

"I know," Phillips answered. "That's why these situations are always so tense. Even the best case situation has a plethora of holes in it, and things can go bad, quick. Whoever these suspects are, they had to know their chances of getting away increased exponentially with the hostage."

"And worst case scenario?" Before Michael could answer, Chloe continued. "I'm almost afraid to ask."

"Worst case scenario..." Phillips grabbed his chin and stroked it slightly as he contemplated the answer.

"Worst case scenario. High-speed chase. Accidents because the highway isn't clear. Spike strip effective or ineffective. Ineffective, and the assailants don't slow down. Their car crashes killing everyone inside. Effective, their car is disabled, the police have them surrounded. The situation escalates and ends in a gunfight."

Chloe's eyes widened with each component of Michael's description.

"I don't think I like either of those scenarios, best or worst."

"We can only hope for the best," Michael suggested.

The radio cracked, and the two paused to listen in on the details.

"Looks like they are heading our way," Michael said. "Buckle up."

"They perched up," Major warned as their car passed the school. "You see' em up top?"

"Yeah, I got' em," Mayven replied as she moved forward. At the end of the street was a four-way stop. The light was red. They had to wait, with the police on their left side at the school, and officers positioned in squad cars on their right. The tension was so thick, an ordinary knife couldn't cut it. The anxiety-ridden situation wasn't good for Mr. Franklin. His wheezing was the only sound that could be heard in the car while they waited for the light to turn green.

"I need my inhaler," he wheezed.

His plea was ignored. The light turned green. Livingston ordered the officers on Barrett Parkway to follow but at a distance with no sirens or hot lights. Mayven turned the corner and pointed the car in the direction of the interstate. The police cars waited a beat and fell in behind them. All other traffic was supposed to be held back, but something had gone awry. A media truck fell in behind the culprits, and then other cars turned onto the thoroughfare. Now, there were multiple vehicles on the three-lane road moving in the same direction as the assailants. A couple of squad cars tracking the attackers lost visual and alerted the chief. Livingston hesitated. The helicopters were in position, but they would have to turn on lights in order to track the car. The sight of the helicopters could be enough to cause the suspects to panic. Livingston didn't want that with so many pedestrian cars around. The quandaries for the Chief continued to escalate.

Detective Phillips was ready. He had both hands on the steering wheel and repeatedly checked his rearview mirror for the car the suspects were in, a Black Charger with South Carolina license plates, with a woman driver.

"South Carolina plates, more than one assailant," Chloe repeated. She looked at Michael as he turned to look at her.

"Do you think these are the same suspects for the Carolina murders?"

"Makes sense, doesn't it?" He mused.

"Multiple perpetrators, one smaller than the other," Chloe said.

"Two different weapons. We don't have any confirmation of that though," Michael thought.

"Yeah, but what are the chances?" Chloe asserted.

"Right. What are the chances," Michael repeated.

There was one more traffic light between Mayven and Major and the interstate. The Charger was blanketed by other cars which offered a buffer between them and the police. Cornelius looked out of the passenger side window, recognizing places he passed every day going to and coming from work. Each time a car slowed down near him, he tried to make eye contact with the driver. Somebody needed to know he was in a dire situation so they could help him.

"Please, can you let the window down so I can get some air? I can barely breathe," he uttered painfully. The blood around his nose had long since dried. There was still pain that migrated, giving him a pronounced headache. That combined with his severe asthmatic condition and no medicine to fix it, Cornelius was in bad shape. His pronounced wheezing was a huge distraction for Mayven. She lifted her hip enough to pull his medicine from his back pocket.

"Dose him," she said, handing the inhaler to Major. "He won't do us any good dead."

For the slightest moment, Major removed the gun from Cornelius' temple and flipped the cap off the inhaler.

"Open up," he said, jamming the dispenser in Mr. Franklins' mouth. Cornelius pulled hard as Major depressed the button that released the Albuterol. As the medication started to relieve the constriction Cornelius felt in his chest, he cut his eyes in Major's direction signaling the need for more. Feeling generous, Major compressed the button once again and coated the hostages' airway with the medication. Mr. Franklin's chest rose and fell hard and then it began to ease as the medicine started to work. Major didn't bother to put the cap back on the dispenser, opting instead to toss it on the back seat so he could retrieve his gun. He never wanted Mr. Franklin to think for one minute that the threat to his life wasn't real.

This time when the cool steel of the muzzle was placed against his temple, Mr. Franklin didn't wince. Instead, he accepted that this was the situation, for now. At least he could breathe for the moment. Traffic slowed as drivers began to position themselves for the next stretch.

"Left or right, bae," Mayven asked looking for confirmation from Major.

"Right," he answered. "Take it downtown."

Mayven didn't bother to put the blinker on but forced her way over to the furthest right-hand land closest to the on-ramp for Interstate 285. Michael picked up the movement in his rearview mirror. He called out on the intercom that he had the suspect car in sight.

"Stay with them Phillips but keep your distance," Chief Livingston warned.

"Yes sir," Michael replied, releasing the speak button on the intercom system. "Get ready Chloe; I don't know how this is going to go."

Chloe readjusted her seatbelt. She looked in the side mirror, but her positioning didn't allow her the same vantage point Michael had. She thought for a minute and took out her phone. If they did end up in a high-speed chase, Chloe didn't want Addison seeing it played out on television with no advanced warning. Chloe sent a quick text with a caveat.

Don't panic. Still with Phillips. I am okay. High-speed chase pending. Don't freak out... and don't obsess over the news. Will check in when I can.

Even as Chloe hit send, she knew Addison well enough to know that panicking is exactly what she would do no matter what the message said. But she promised to check in and with the forewarning, all Chloe could hope is that Addison wouldn't take a dive off the deep end. Chloe's phone chirped almost as fast as the message was sent.

OMG! Okay... I will try not to panic... thanks for the heads up... please be careful... please...

Confirmation that at least a partial panic was already in effect. Chloe smiled slightly as she replaced her cell phone in her jacket pocket. She looked over at Detective Phillips. He had his game face on. She had never seen him in the heat of battle like this before; always arriving at the scene when the action was over. Something about his intensity and a fond remembrance of their kiss was very sexy.

"Addison good?" Michael asked, taking a second to look in Chloe's direction.

"As well as she can be," Chloe answered.

Michael smiled with Chloe. While they still had a moment, he reached over and placed his hand on her leg. When she covered his with her own, Michael's smile grew. With a gentle squeeze, he let her know everything was going to be okay. It was a reminder that he would lay it all on the line for her. Chloe felt that instinctively.

Michael replaced his hand on the steering wheel as the light changed. He was taking a gamble with the way he was positioned. The suspects could try and access the highway going in the opposite direction, but they hadn't. They fell right in line, right where his car was positioned.

"Here they come," Michael said as the charge passed them. Chloe lifted herself from the passenger seat and tried to look past Michael to get a look at the assailants. Chloe barely caught a glimpse of the person on the passenger's side. But as the car made it onto the on-ramp, and lights from oncoming cars illuminated the way, she got a brief look inside. It wasn't enough for her to discern one from two or anything like that but the passenger turned his head sufficiently enough for her to see his profile.

Michael eased the truck out into traffic. The truck was positioned less than 100 feet from the on-ramp, so it didn't take long before they were ascending onto the interstate behind the escaping vehicle. It was hard for Michael to lay back. His instinct was to chase and apprehend. But there were too many factors, vulnerabilities he couldn't control. He would follow, at a safe distance, and report in as the situation unfolded. Michaels pursuing vehicle was not alone. Chief Livingston wanted the culprits to know that the police were present, so there were a number of marked and unmarked cars moving through traffic and tracking the vehicle. 'Big Bertha', APD's mobile control center, also followed the convoy of pursuing officers. Construction on Interstate 285 by Cumberland Mall was a bottleneck when traffic was high. If that was the case, things could slow up, and the suspects could get antsy. Nervous suspects would not make for a good situation.

The Charger was moving fast, weaving in and out of traffic. When the racing car cut off some driver, the offended driver laid on the horn. Fortunately or unfortunately, 285 was relatively clear, and the suspects, as well as the police, moved unencumbered.

"They've got a decision to make," Michael said as he moved the vehicle at a steady clip to keep up.

"What decision is that," Chloe asked with a cautious hand placed on the dashboard.

"The Highway 20 connector is coming up, fastest way downtown."

Chief Livingston was tracking the situation as well. The police copters were up and following the assailants. That would be the quickest way for him to get information on which way they were headed. If they took the 20 exit, police were positioned ten miles ahead and could get the spike strips out hopefully in time. The problem with these kinds of situations was the ancillary traffic and the number of contingencies. It was all hands on deck. The police were busy on 20, 85, and Langford Parkway and every other major thoroughfare trying to anticipate what the culprits would do next.

Major and Mayven both felt the heat. Police were everywhere. Masterfully, Mayven moved the car through traffic. The police had yet to light up their chase lights, but Mayven felt like that could happen at any moment. Still, she didn't panic. Instead, she kept her head in the game and drove. Mayven kept the car in the middle of the highway. Too far to either side could compel the police to try and pull her over. She pushed the speed limit but not more than any other driver around her. For all practical purposes, they were just like everyone else; except they had a hostage, and weapons, and blood on their hands.

Suddenly, Mayven crossed two lanes to make the transition from one highway to another. Detective Phillips saw the car exit 285, and he pursued. The other police cars fell in behind his SUV, and the chase continued. Livingston got the word that the suspects were now traveling west on Interstate 20. He called ahead to the officers standing by to prepare for the spike strips. Dr. Daniels heart was pumping. Being on this side of the action was starkly different than anything she'd experienced before. The scenarios Michael described before played out vividly in her mind. Chloe wasn't sure how this would end, whether Michael would be right or not. All she could do at this point was hold on and hope for the best for everyone involved.

Officers worked diligently, narrowing the traffic lanes to give the fleeing suspects fewer options and shutting down the highway from the on-ramp to where the spike strips were to be placed. The police had to be smart and decrease opportunities for the assailants to exit the highway in anticipation of police interference. Although risky, Livingston gave the command for squad cars with flashers on to block the exits down Interstate 20. Unlike many of the major thoroughfares in Atlanta, 20 didn't have the kind of congestion especially in the wee hours of the morning. The police caught a break in that there wasn't a whole lot of ancillary traffic to deal with. Everybody stood at the ready in preparation for the Charger's arrival.

Mayven hit the on-ramp on 20. It didn't take long before orange cones, and flashing lights and vacant highway greeted them.

"This shit bout to be deep," Major said, leaning forward and scoping out their surroundings. It didn't take long before the downtown skyscrapers came into view. Cornelius was breathing better, but his heart nearly beat out of his chest. There was an overwhelming sense of foreboding even though he was a man of faith. He could see no win in this situation for him. At some point, Mr. Franklin would outlive his usefulness, and either of the two of his captors would take his life without a second thought. That he knew for sure.

As the lane options grew slimmer, Mayven had no choice but to comply with the restrictions law enforcement put in their path.

"No matter what they do May, keep driving," Major instructed.

"Got it, bae," she confirmed.

As they rounded a wide curve, the merge options for Interstate 85 came into view. And then they heard it, a loud bullhorn or mechanism of some sort instructing them to stop. Lights swirled in red and blue frenzy; officers lined both sides of the highway. Exits were blocked off. Mayven's eyes swelled as the Chargers' headlights picked up an object being tossed across the lane she had no choice but to drive in. The cars' lights amplified the silvery spikes on the strip.

Mayven looked over her shoulder to Major. He nodded and she pressed on the gas. Cornelius saw it too; steel to his temple, steel tips in their path. With his hands bound, there was nothing he could do to brace himself against what was to come. All he could do was steeple the fingers on his bound wrists and whisper a silent word of prayer. The Chargers rate of speed increased as the assailants approached the strip. Calls continued to come out from the bullhorn demanding that they stop. Everything seemed to happen in slow motion as the swiftly rotating tires of the Charger met the iron spikes designed to womb and puncture them. Detective Phillips truck was a few hundred feet behind. He had the benefit of forewarning about the strips and instead of speeding up he slowed the truck down. Michael had been there before.

The squad cars lining the road and blocking the exit presented a challenge for all oncoming police officers. They would have to be stealthy in their navigation and pursuit of the assailants once the strips were activated. Media helicopters and police copters lit the night sky separate from the distant lights of downtown Atlanta. People were tuned into their television sets, perched on the edge of their seats watching their own OJ Simpson Bronco chase play out. But this time the Charger moved fast. There were three people in the car, and one was a hostage. Addison was amongst those glued to the news channels. This was more than breaking news. For Addison, this news was personal. Her boss was a part of the chase.

The news commentary was play by play like watching a major sports event instead of a true crime story. Correspondents talked about the possibilities, the 'what could happen next' of the situation. They still didn't have names for the assailants, but they knew Mr. Cornelius Franklin was in the suspects' car. The problem was, nobody got a good look at the suspects, and Devereux was still off limits. It was a crime scene. Everybody waited with eyes wide and hearts pumping to see how this would all play out.

Mayven was fearless. Everything she was ever afraid of, Mayven already lived through. As the Charger rolled over the pointy spikes, there was loud popping as at least two of the tires caught the full force and the rubber tread was punctured. Mr. Franklin's breathing grew more labored, and Major held the gun as firmly in his hand as possible when the car shook from the impact. But Mayven did what Major told her to do. She kept driving even though she could feel the stability of the tires weakening.

Officers responsible for the spike strip did their best to remove it as quickly as possible to avoid damaging the police cars that had fallen back. Once the strip was out of the way, those tracking the Charger accelerated to close the distance between them. Detective Phillips' SUV was one of those vehicles. Chloe heard the car hit the strip and watched as it continued down the highway. The impact to the tires was undeniable.

"They're still going" was the comment of several of the news reporters. But it wouldn't be for long. The Chargers tires couldn't stand up under the tears created by the spikes, and despite Mayven's best effort, the Charger began to hobble as one tire and then the next flattened out. Within minutes, the Charger was immobile, and the police closed in, surrounding the assailants on all sides. This was the moment of truth. The helicopters overhead positioned themselves and then hovered with spotlights illuminating the broken down vehicle. Officers exited their vehicles and turned their standard issued weapons in the direction of the assailants' car. Detective Phillips pulled the SUV to the side of the road; close enough to advance on foot but far enough back to not put Dr. Daniels at greater risk.

"Stay inside," he commanded as he opened the door and took out his weapon. "Do not get out of this car, understand?"

Phillips didn't wait for a response. He had to move. Squatting as he ran, Phillips positioned himself behind a squad car alongside officers who already had their weapons locked in on the culprits. Mayven put the car in park but didn't bother to turn off the ignition. She grabbed her knife from off the passenger floor boards. Major looked around and surveyed their surroundings.

"Looks like we got ourselves a motherfuckin standoff..."

Well, actually, to be continued in part five of the Chloe Daniels Mysteries, RUN!

Thank you so much for reading and stay tuned!

Note from the Author

Thank you so much for reading FIT: the 4th installment in the Chloe Daniels Mysteries! I hope you enjoyed it and plan to continue along with this crazy bunch of characters! Reviews are the life blood of independent writers. The more reviews we get, the more Amazon and others promote the book. If you want to see more Chloe Daniels Mysteries, a review would go a long way towards allowing me to write more books. If you liked the book, I ask you to write a review of Run on Amazon.com, Goodreads or where ever you go for your book information. Thank you so much. Doing so means a lot to me. If you didn't like the book, then please disregard this paragraph.

More Books by Deidra D.S. Green:

- **The Twisted Sister Trilogy**
- Twisted Sister (book 1)
- Twisted's Revenge (Book 2)
- After the Twist (Book 3)
- **Woman at the Top of the Stairs Trilogy**
- Woman at the Top of the Stairs (Book 1)
- Sweetest Revenge (Book 2)
- The Final Say (Book 3)
- Suddenly Single: So Undeserving
- **The Chloe Daniel's Mysteries**

- <u>Sick, Sicker, Sickest: (The 1st installment in the Chloe Daniels Mysteries)</u>
- <u>HUSH: (The 2nd installment in Chloe Daniels)</u>
- <u>Mischief's Mayhem: (The 3rd installment in Chloe Daniels)</u>
- FIT: (The 4th Installment in Chloe Daniels)
- RUN (the 5th installment in Chloe Daniels)
- <u>Ivy: Some Say she's Poison</u>
- <u>Interstate 64</u>
- <u>My Guy Friday</u>
- <u>Elite Affairs I: Orchestrated Beauty</u>
- <u>Elite Affairs II: Simple Elegance</u>

Check out Deidra's Amazon page
amzn.to/2nqi3iG

Grab a personalized copy at
<u>bit.ly/readwithDDSG</u>

Get a free e-book when you subscribe to Deidra's newsletter!
<u>https://www.instafreebie.com/free/Vev7x</u>